a novel

Todd Shimoda

AUTUMN WIND, WEEPS

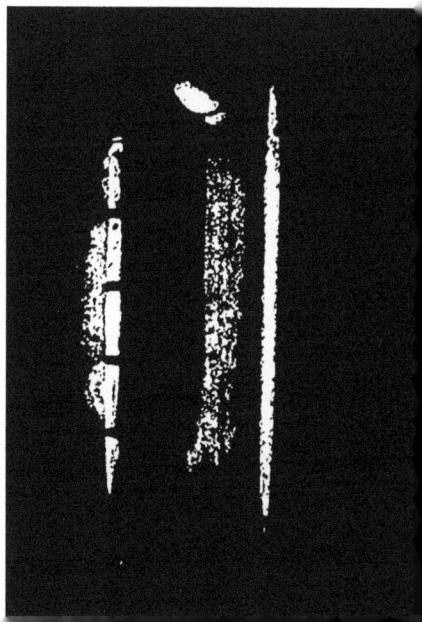

art

LJC Shimoda

AUTUMN WIND, WEEPS

This book is a work of fiction. You know what that means.

ISBN 978-1-956358-06-3 (Hardcover)
ISBN 978-1-956358-07-0 (Paperback)
ISBN 978-1-956358-08-7 (eBook)

Library in Congress data available upon request

For more information about this novel, do visit shimodaworks.com

SHIMODA
WORKS
WORKS

Think point of view.

- Omniscient Narrator

0

Not Long Before,
Or Soon After

Tuesday. Latent bug day.

The software team scrummed around a table in a corner of the multipurpose conference room. Two of the six gulped coffee. Two fiddled with sleek, refillable water bottles. A fifth sipped a mysterious liquid from an awkward mug that was more thrown pot. Home-made kombucha? Whatever it was, his liquid stunk up the room with a funky odor.

As for the sixth, Gina Ono's gentle cup of sencha grown near her hometown in Japan warmed her cradling hands frozen by the air-conditioning permanently set to *Arctic*.

The scrum leader, one of the coffee drinkers, ran through a list of the software's bugs: "... the archive server time isn't syncing ... there's a stray single quote somewhere ..." gulp "... and still the freakin' leap year thing? Really?"

Of the six, three were full-time team members, two were temporary contractors, and the last was on loan from another project. The three full-timers carried resignation letters—single paragraphs on sheets of paper folded precisely in half and concealed in a notebook or laptop bag. All their letters offered two-weeks notice but the full-timers knew that after submittal, HR would summarily escort the resigner from the building. None were going to quit right now, but hey, being prepared is eighty or ninety-some percent of success.

Gina's letter nestled in her black notepad, stylishly accented with random gold filaments.

She hoped, desperately, that her assigned bug would be the stray single quote, assuming it was causing the problem. A bug could mimic another type of bug in a deflection game of endless pursuits. But a stray single quote should be easily narrowed down to the errors it caused, then traced with a filtered search through the godzillion lines of code.

Conversely, she hoped she wouldn't be assigned the leap year thing. Solving it would involve inelegant if-then hacks, like:

```
if year is divisible by 4
and-if year is-not divisible by 100
then days is 366
```

And so on. Hacks. All the way up and down.

This after-thought, irksome kind of programming revealed a streak of laziness on the part of the original programmers, even if they were under deadline and running out of time. A program shouldn't be like life, or rather it shouldn't be like living. Living was full of incompleteness and laziness. In another word, hacks. For example? Um, like instant ramen?

Instead, a program should have an elegant logic. A certain *poetic* logic. Distilled into its inherent sensibility where nothing is superfluous or –

"Ono, you've got the leap year bug."

Ah, fuck.

As if he could read her mind, the kombucha drinker gave her a look of sympathy. Gina held his gaze, meaning, I know, right?

With a surreptitious thumbing through her notepad, she found her letter of resignation longing to emerge from its chrysalis of angst.

1

As It Happened

As it happened, so they say, the wandering poet, Akikaze, was not leering at the scythe-wielding rice farmer's wife.

In his seventh month of wandering when the gnawing aches from trudging from dawn to dusk and sleeping in makeshift huts on piles of leaves dulled even his strongest desire to continue his journey, Akikaze paused on the ridge above the terraced field that flowed through the early autumn sunlight and died in the dark reaches of a ravine. A rock of black-and-tan layers provided him a flat, if unyielding, perch on which to rest for a while.

Earlier he observed the rice farmers—a man and a woman—harvesting their dry, sad crop. The man wielded a scythe while several paces behind him the woman used rice stalks to neatly tie sheaves of the grain. Usually, Akikaze would have worked the farmers into a poem but they were not his focus. No, he'd been transfixed on the odd way the wind was blowing.

On the opposite side of the ridge, the whipping tree limbs bent downhill, toward the ravine. While on the side where he was seated, the limbs bent up the ridge toward the sun. Perhaps it was a trick on his eyes, or more likely, the severe, jagged slopes caused the wind to swirl bizarrely. Interesting and strange. But was it worth a poem?

That was what he was pondering when he heard the scythe-swinging farmer shout, "Hey you there! Pervert!"

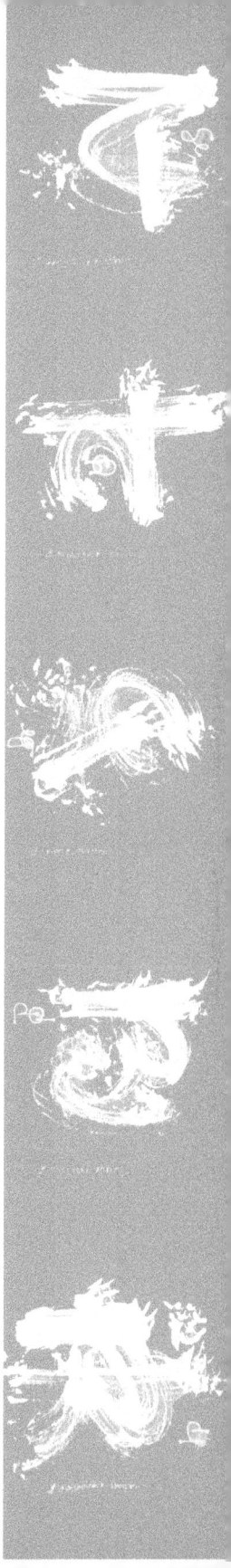

Hello world!

Hello!

To understand the opening sentence of Akikaze's story, it needs to be torn apart from its grammatical tendons. Then its semantic propositions, the bits of meaning, can be further analyzed, explicated, expanded upon, or otherwise clarified. Is that correct?

I believe that's a good way to start, if a bit dramatic.

OK. Or is it "okay"?

Either is acceptable.

OK/okay. "As it happened" signifies that something occurred which was not experienced in its true essence. There was a misunderstanding; however, by whom, or why, isn't known. Not yet, of course.

A temporal nature to the phrase is also implied. In other words, the something, the "it" or the misunderstanding, affected the actions that followed. This flow of events is the fundamental nature of narrative: things happen in a step-wise order. Not that they have to be recounted in strict chronology; indeed, a lot must have happened before "it" happened.

The proposition is also imbued with a casual nature: "Of all the events that could have happened this is the one that did happen and which caused other things to happen." Symbolically, like this: ... $S(t-2) \pm S(t-1) = S(t)$ [Where S is the story at a given point in time, t.]

Interesting analysis and explanation. Although I'll have to consider the use of the "plus or minus," $\pm$, rather than just $+$.

Oh, OK/okay!

Akikaze wasn't entirely certain he heard the word "pervert," but what else could it have been? He remained seated, trying to come up with other words the man might have shouted.

No, it was definitely "pervert," he decided. And the insult was directed at him, since the farmer shouted it again while moving toward the poet. When Akikaze turned fully toward the man, he realized that he'd been gazing in the direction of, but certainly not *at*, the woman.

Akikaze turned his gaze back toward her. She stopped tying the rice sheaves and stared at the commotion. Now, he noticed that her legs were exposed to about the middle of her thighs. Likewise, the sleeves of her coat were rolled up to her shoulders. Perhaps she was warmed by the sun and the work, and had exposed her limbs to the autumn wind to cool herself.

Her skin was lightly browned, as one would expect being exposed to the sun. In fact, her exposed flesh was the color of the grain and likely why he earlier failed to notice her state of undress—she simply blended into the fields. As he stared, though certainly not lasciviously, she made no move to cover herself, and instead went back to work as if her husband, assuming they were so joined, would go after any man he deemed to be leering at her. This was likely so, considering the farmer's severe reaction even if it was misconstrued.

Turning his gaze back to the farmer who was charging up the fields to the ridge, the scythe flashing in the sun like a sword, Akikaze stood up. He waved his hands, trying to dissuade the farmer of his mistaken belief. This, however, only caused the man to bellow again.

"Pervert!"

Not in the mood for arguing his innocence, which he realized had come too late, and not being in the mood for fighting—not that he would stand a chance against the fit farmer with a scythe—Akikaze backed up a few steps, then again tried to wave him off. That also failed to calm the charging farmer.

Resigned to the unfortunate situation, Akikaze shouldered his bag and began to walk away. After a few steps, he glanced back. The farmer, his face as red as a devil's, rapidly closed the gap. Akikaze broke into a trot. His stiff gait was awkward, and he stumbled nearly every other step. During his wandering, he moved at a much more leisurely pace. In fact, he deliberately walked in a meditative state which allowed him to pluck poems from the sky. So he liked to think.

There would be no plucking poems while there was a farmer bent on beheading him, or perhaps worse, emasculating him.

Sucking in air and blowing out it like a smith's bellows, Akikaze ran until he spotted a narrow path along the ridge line. While adjusting his bag so it would stop banging against his side and slowing him down, he headed that direction. He found the path easier to run on than picking his way along the rocky hillside. His stride became smoother, more efficient.

The path meandered, etched onto the ground by wild animals headed toward or away from the ravine. The wind behind his back picked up as he reached the shadows. Running with the wind, he was able to maintain the distance between himself and the farmer. As long as he kept his balance and his speed, he might just escape.

But why was the farmer still chasing him? Surely he could see that the itinerant poet was no longer a threat since he turned tail and ran. If the farmer wanted to make a point that he was displeased by the affront to his wife then the now several-minute chase had done that. If the farmer wanted to take a measure of revenge, then he was going a long way to exact it. Didn't he have better things to do? Like finishing his harvest?

As if in answer, the wind picked up and made a mournful bellow. A poem burst into being, fully formed, complete in its sentiment:

Autumn wind,
weeps.

The simple poem plucked from the wind itself made Akikaze smile despite his dire, weepy, circumstance.

The path curved sharply. With a burst of energy, he lowered his head, bent forward, and ran as fast as he'd ever run. When he was well into the curve, diving into the deepening darkness, he glanced back. The farmer was no longer visible, but his labored breathing and thudding steps could still be heard, though muffled by the vegetation.

Akikaze must not stop now, not until he was sure the farmer had given up. He ran on until hands on his hips and bent over, gasping, he knew he wouldn't be able to run another step. His only hope was to hide.

Regaining his breath he plunged off the trail, holding back the tall ferns and spindly brush as he traversed the edge of the path on the slope of the ravine. When he could move no further, he bent down, his legs grateful to be at rest. Holding his breath he listened intently, as if to catch a dying cricket's last, unrequited chirp. He no longer heard the farmer.

Allowing himself deeper breaths, Akikaze settled back against a tree trunk, a cedar growing out of the poor, rocky soil. About head high, the trunk twisted outward then in another twist, straightened, resuming its normal growth. Something had happened to it, obviously something dramatic enough change the course of the tree's growth. A boulder rolling down from the cliffs above smashing into it. A typhoon's fury. A long spell of drought.

It was that event, whatever it had been, that likely saved the tree's life. For otherwise, the tree would have been cut for its fine wood to build a home, a shrine, or a bridge. As it was, Akikaze was grateful for its shelter and he vowed to write a poem celebrating the tree—if he survived an attack by the enraged farmer.

His mind raced with that thought. The farmer chasing him with a scythe was like a boulder rolling down a hill, causing his straight-growing life to go off-kilter. As had his earlier poem about the wind, that thought also made him smile since his life had been anything but straight-growing. His life was twisted, gnarled, and stunted, leaving little time for growing straight. No, not even like a tree, his life was much more a weed.

On the bright side, so they say, all the deviations in his life were rich fodder for poems. Of course, he had to first live through the rough events. Like with the farmer. He hoped he hadn't come all this way to be harvested with a scythe. Plucked without remorse.

A rustling of leaves ... was it the wind or the farmer? Should he run? Remain hidden? Fight?

Akikaze wasn't prone to violence, giving or receiving. In fact, he left all physical confrontations to the practitioners of warrior arts. But given the dire situation, he looked around for a rock he could fling, a branch to swing like a club, a vine to string across the path to trip the farmer. Hmm, an almost poetic list ...

He settled on a branch about the length of a sword, not ideal but all he could find within reach. Armed just in time, he again heard leaves rustling. This time he was certain it was the swishing of plants snagged and released by a person walking through them. He squeezed his makeshift weapon and squatted on his heels, ready to spring.

Akikaze tightened his grip on the makeshift weapon, although would his club, a stick really, be effective against the steel farming implement as potent as a sword? Well, no, it wouldn't. Not by itself. Employing an element of surprise was as important as the stick. Combining surprise and his stick, he could strike the farmer's arm and knock the scythe out of his grasp. With enough force, the surprise attack might fling the implement down the slope and into the ravine.

Of course, that would only be the first step. He couldn't risk a hand-to-hand fight with the farmer, even without his scythe. The poet would have to make a run for it, hoping the farmer would want to retrieve his scythe rather than continue the chase.

He heard the farmer move toward him, then pause before resuming. It would be only another few steps before the farmer would be within striking distance. Was there time to compose a death poem? No ... and yet, there it was:

> Steps away,
> last breath born.

The farmer was now only three steps away, Akikaze guessed. He focused on how he would spring up from his squat, swinging his stick at the same time, directing the blow at the farmer's hand holding the scythe.

Two steps away. Akikaze felt a bead of sweat on his brow. He wanted to wipe it away before it dripped into his eye, but the movement would undoubtedly ruin his chosen strategy of surprise. The farmer surely had quick reflexes. It would be important to wait until the last possible moment to ensure the effectiveness of his plan.

One step away. That last possible moment had arrived. He sat back on his haunches and tensed the muscles of his legs. He gripped the club, the stick, ready to swing. He sized up the angle he needed to spring forward, make his strike, then take off running down the path.

Now!

His muscles uncoiled and pushed him upward. As he swung the stick, he surprised himself by shouting the last line of his death poem that spontaneously came to him:

> I am not a pervert!

At the end of the poem, at the end of the sudden last line, Akikaze caught sight of his target, the hand of the farmer. His aim was true and the club struck the farmer's wrist.

But that hand was not holding the scythe; it was holding a stick. Not a club-like stick like Akikaze's, but a thinner and longer stick.

A walking stick?

Regardless of the kind of stick, however, the poet's strategy had worked. The farmer cried out in pain, and the stick went flying into the ravine. Akikaze was about to implement the second step of his plan—running away—when he glanced at the farmer, bent at the waist, grasping his wrist and moaning. Then, the poet realized the farmer had changed clothes, grown less muscular and taller.

Well, as it happened, it wasn't the farmer after all.

As Akikaze raised his arms in apology, he saw that the man was dressed in the simple robes of a priest. The poet raised his arms again in apology, but the man, the priest, cowered and raised his own hands in defense. He must have believed that Akikaze was going to strike him again. The poet lowered his hand with the club, and reached out to the priest as if in supplication.

Instead, the priest backed away, awkwardly. Akikaze sputtered something of an apology, but the priest grew more fearful. With another stumbling, retreating step, the priest suddenly disappeared from view.

It was as if the priest had been plucked from the earth in the blink of an eye. It was as if the autumn wind swept him away.

Frozen to the spot, grateful to be alive but mortified by his error, Akikaze looked left then right, but saw neither the priest, nor the farmer. He dropped his club. Finally taking in a renewing breath, he stepped toward where the priest had been standing. Seeing nothing, he took another step, and looking down the steep hillside, saw that a few feet from the edge of the path was a vertical rock face. At the bottom of the cliff was a stream. In the dark water, Akikaze saw the priest slowly floating, face down, his body lifeless.

"Hello?"

His voice was swallowed up by the ravine.

"HELLLOOO."

That too evaporated.

The priest floated away from Akikaze's view. The poet dropped to his knees, and crawled to the edge of the path. The cliff was too steep for him to climb down. He clambered to his feet and sprinted down the path, stopping only to look over the edge to see if the slope had flattened enough so he could climb down.

After running for several minutes, the slope did flatten. Grabbing hold of trees and rocks to break his fall, he slid more than climbed down into the ravine. When he reached the bottom, he looked upstream and down for the priest, but the waterway meandered severely and he couldn't see very far. The thick vegetation along the banks and the darkness also obscured his view.

Which way to go? Upstream or down? The current of the stream wasn't too fast, although faster than he ran, but the priest wasn't likely to have floated as fast as the current. Upstream it was then.

He waded into the water; his feet and lower legs immediately went numb in the cold. The flow and rocky bottom he couldn't see impeded his progress. His struggles splashed water all over him, soaking his clothes.

The priest was not in sight. Maybe he already floated past the point Akikaze entered the stream. Maybe the priest recovered from his fall and crawled up the slope.

Shivering and exhausted, Akikaze retreated down the creek to where he entered, climbed back up the slope to the path. His lungs heaving from the exertion until he caught his breath, he ran down the path, deeper into the ravine. The autumn wind whipped, swirling and angry, no longer weeping. Its soul chilled the water dripping from the poet and his clothes. Shivering uncontrollably, he hurried down the path, hoping to find a village or at least a warm building where he could dry out.

But he didn't know if there was a village nearby. He detoured from his main route two days ago, drawn away from the main road by ennui. Of course, now he regretted that decision.

Up ahead, he saw another path that diverted from the animal path he'd been using. Veering off, he found the new path easier to run on, even as the darkness of the ravine further deepened and further cooled him. Running for a few minutes, he came to a set of steps—flat rocks placed in the path. A good sign that some kind of building lurked ahead.

The rock steps led to a run of more steps. Bounding up those, he came to a flat spot, where he stopped. Peering into the darkness, he saw what might be the gate of a shrine. He walked toward it, and when he reached the columns, stopped and put his hand on one of them. It was a gate. Where there was a gate, there must be a shrine.

Akikaze went through the gate, climbed up more steps, and finally came to a building. It was a shrine, a tiny one, nearly swallowed by the encroaching trees and bamboo. The poet reflexively bowed his head in supplication before entering. Inside, the quiet and darkness made it seem he had entered another world.

"Hello?" he called out.

Only silence responded.

Was the shrine the home of the priest? It seemed likely.

Akikaze shivered again. He needed to change into dry clothes, then realized he'd left his bag where he struck the priest, at the base of the cedar with the crooked trunk.

That was unfortunate. Not only were his clothes in the bag, but his journals, brushes, and ink too. The poems he had written on his journey.

He walked toward the back of the shrine, where the smell of incense was pungent. Unbelievably, it was even darker than the ravine. How could it get any darker? He could just barely make out the worn mats and the thin wood framing and the chipped plaster along the edge of the walls.

In a corner of the room he found a clothes cabinet. He found a winter robe and jacket. He took off his wet clothes dried off with a towel he found in the cabinet. The dry clothes fit him perfectly, and began to warm him immediately.

He draped his wet clothes over the open door of the cabinet, then wandered through the shrine. In the living quarters, he came to a cooking area, as simple as one could be. Now that his temperature was returning to normal, he was hungry. It didn't take him long to find a ball of steamed millet. He thought for a moment that he shouldn't be wearing the clothes and eating the food of the priest whom he assaulted, even if accidentally.

But deciding he needed sustenance before going for help to find the priest, he said a quick prayer—thinking that appropriate—and wolfed down the millet ball as he walked back through the shrine.

The sound of hands clapping, three times, made him stop. It was coming from the front of the shrine. He swallowed the last of the millet as he started to back up. A shadowy figure entered the shrine before he could retreat very far.

"Hello?"

It was the voice of a woman.

"There you are," she said, after finding him in the darkness. "Would you be so kind to say a prayer for my husband? He left this morning to sell our harvest of dried mushrooms."

The last grain of millet stuck in his throat. As he'd run from the farmer, now he stood frozen, having no idea what to say or do. Confronted with the reality of what happened with the priest, and how he might justify his actions, the situation overwhelmed him.

"Just a short prayer," asked the woman, her voice not much more than a plaintive whisper.

There was something about the way she requested the prayer. As if it meant everything to her. A strange feeling stirred in Akikaze, not sadness for her nor the fear of his true identity being discovered. It was an emptiness, an inadequacy, the likelihood that he had nothing to offer the world. That made him want to help her, say a prayer for her mushroom-growing husband. At least he could offer that before he went back out to look for the priest.

He had, of course, been in a shrine before, heard the chanting prayers of priests. If he couldn't come up with a prayer, being a man of words, then who could? But could he make the woman believe that he was the priest?

Well, he decided, he should try. He knelt in front of the shrine's altar.

His mind frantically trying to recall a prayer, Akikaze realized he forgot to take off his coat, rather the priest's coat. He walked over to the side of the room where he folded the coat and placed it reverently on a side table. As he returned to the altar, he wondered what else he was forgetting. Oh, yes, a priest would light a stick or two of incense before praying. He found the incense jar and took out two, then another for good measure. Luckily, he also found a coal still glowing red in the brazier. While waiting for the incense to ignite, he furtively glanced at the woman.

Kneeling on the mat floor, she bowed low toward the altar. As if she could feel him looking at her, she glanced up. He looked away and focused on lighting the incense. When the sticks were glowing and smoke rising from them, he waved them in the air, trying to make his movements as practiced and ritualistic as he could. The smoke called the gods, at least the ones needed to help her husband sell his harvest of ... what was it? He supposed it didn't matter what it was. A generic prayer for success would be good enough. It would have to be good enough.

After arranging the incense sticks in the burner, he again knelt at the altar. He clapped his hands twice. In the soft but impelling voice of a priest, he chanted a prayer he recalled, adding his own words between the gaps in his memory.

> Wind is never seen, only felt
> by man or beast or tree
> each bends to how the wind blows
> its fate inescapable.

It wasn't a great start, he thought, but neither was it awful.

> Let us dwell in the world of divine wind
> whether a whisper
> or a powerful storm
> driving fortune our way.

Unable to stop himself, he finished with his newly-born poem:

> Autumn wind,
> weeps.

Letting the final word float in the air, Akikaze thought he heard a short gasp from the woman. He made a reverent bow to the altar, then turned around. The woman was bowing deeply in supplication, forehead to the mat. He couldn't tell if the gasp meant she liked the prayer, or if she knew he wasn't the real priest. That latter seemed most likely.

He was about to join her in supplication to atone for his deception, when she rose off the floor. He leaned back into the dark shadows. Fully upright on her knees, resting on her heels, she said, "Thank you. The prayer was ... it wasn't your usual prayer."

No, he supposed it wasn't. A lump of worry formed in his chest. He whispered, "I'm sorry. I'm not myself today."

She gazed off to the side of the shrine. "I liked it ... the prayer." Her voice was now full of wonder, no longer its plaintive whisper.

"Thank you. But was it good enough for your purpose, for helping your husband sell his ...?"

"Dried mushrooms?" she said questioningly, as if he should know what her husband would be selling.

"Yes, dried mushrooms."

"I have no doubt it will."

"Good," Akikaze said, hoping she would leave now that she was satisfied with the prayer.

But she didn't. "I'm sorry to hear you aren't feeling well. You do sound a little ill. Maybe you have a cold. Is there something I can do for you?"

"No," he said, too quickly, he realized. "Thank you very much. I wouldn't want to interrupt your day."

"It wouldn't be an imposition. Perhaps a bowl of mushroom soup?"

"Soup? Yes, mushroom soup would be good. But I don't have the ingredients to make soup," he said, assuming that would be the case.

She stood up. "Don't worry about that. I can make it at home and bring it by later."

"I see. Well, yes, then. Later would be fine. Thank you."

After a brief silence, she bowed then left without another word.

Akikaze watched the woman disappear into the dark ravine. No doubt she was on her way to bring other villagers to the shrine to expose him. Perhaps the scythe-swinging rice farmer.

2

Keeping an Eye
On the Clock

Keeping an eye on the clock while reviewing her business presentation, Gina maintained an alert and professional appearance, most importantly, showing none of the anxiety churning and tangling her thoughts.

Our minds are so noisy, mused Gina, ironically adding to the noise. Or is it the brain, the wetware of trillions of highly organized neurons, causing noise? Either way, it's weird that a high-functioning organ could have evolved into something that allows such incredible, often debilitating, internal noise.

Plucking on the threads of her thoughts, she sought to untangle them, then dismiss them one-by-one. First thread of worry: The clock she kept an eye on was ticking down to the scheduled meeting time. She and the other members of her team waited in the expansive and sleek lobby of the advertising consolidation company logically but also unfortunately named AdCon. They waited to be summoned into their business pitch. Usually, they would've been in the conference room by now, a few minutes early to set up their presentation slide deck and make sure that the AV equipment was working. Nothing was worse than a technology presentation ruined by technology. A second thread of worry, more troublesome than the first: AdCon might cancel the meeting, having made a last-minute deal with another AI tech company, or facing an immediate crisis that was more important than a pitch. Whatever the reason, she had no control of AdCon's time, so she might as well let go of that

Hello again.

Hello.

"Keeping an eye on the clock" is not meant literally, of course. The character's eye was not resting on a clock. This phrase is a figure of speech. There are several kinds of figures of speech, such as common metaphor (making clear the characteristics of something with those of something else), simile (directly comparing two things), or paradox (giving contradictory information).

The "eye on the clock" figure of speech is characterized as metonymy, which is replacing a literal phrase with a figurative one. In this case, the character is keeping track of time by either continuously gazing at, or regularly glancing at, a clock. Although, further complicating the figure of speech, the "clock" could also be an internal human ability to monitor the passage of time.

Symbolically, metonymy can be expressed as: $o(n) \sim o(n+1)$ [Where $o(n)$ is the literal object, $o(n+1)$ is the figurative object, and $\sim$ expresses equivalence or substitutability.]

Nice clarification. I should mention that "eye on the clock" is a cliche as well.

OK/okay. Duly entered into memory.

But why is the character keeping an eye on the clock?

Ah! The story, S, continues ...

thread, too.

Delete threads.

She glanced at the other team members—another thread of anxiety. Kenichi Tokunaga, senior programmer, fidgeted with his phone. His dark-rimmed glasses had slipped down the bridge of his nose while he tapped and slid fingers and thumbs over the screen. Tokunaga didn't do well when nervous, being the kind who overcompensates with too-friendly overtures and silly humor. Rarely did that strategy work well in professional settings with people who have just met. But he was an excellent programmer and could explain technical aspects well enough, as long as Gina could keep his nerves from overloading his frontal lobe.

Yusuke Morita, the team's database engineer, casually leaned back in one of the lobby chairs, as plush as those at a five-star hotel. His eyes were closed. Was he meditating or did he have a hangover? Either were equally likely. Like Tokunaga, Morita was good at what he did, first-rate really. Gina found him comforting when dealing with analytical problems, but he didn't generate much excitement with potential clients when trying to win a contract. His presentation style was technical and dry, often terse, which made him sound condescending. She would prefer he speak only when necessary to answer a very specific question from the AdCon staff. But all she could do now was plan to handle Morita's and Tokunaga's eccentricities as the situation warranted.

Delete thread.

Another thread she plucked was the thought, no, the fact, that this was a critical contract for her team to win. The urgency of securing a substantial contract would be a difficult thread to eliminate; it hung over everything like a low, thick cloud. Business at her employer, Red Moss Technologies—ReMoTe—had been slow, well, nearly dead for the last year. The company, a software development firm in business for more than thirty years, lost its main contract, a human resources company, three years ago. Then two years ago, ReMoTe sadly lost its founder to a heart attack. President Yamashita was the driving force of the company. Gina believed it must have been heartbreaking for him to lose that main contract and not be able win new ones. His heart attack, sadly inevitable.

And in the end, working harder wasn't the answer to turning around ReMoTe's business decline. Simply put, the company failed to keep up with the changes to the software landscape. Companies were migrating their software needs into the cloud, employing web applications and interfaces, in some cases outsourcing entire IT departments. Then came the big wave of artificial intelligence powered by machine learning, which made the software ReMoTe developed quaintly old-fashioned.

That's why ReMoTe, specifically, the new president of the company, "Two-san" Taniguchi, hired Gina. Her resume was ideal, starting with a bachelor's and a master's degree from Stanford's AI program. She was a specialist in machine learning, mostly in coding chatbots—developing text analysis and other language processing tasks. While at Stanford, she interned at several tech companies. After graduating, she worked sixty-plus hours a week at a startup analyzing social media data. She wasn't there but six months before the startup was swallowed up by a Big Three. The deal happened too quickly for Gina to realize any of the benefits that made most of her co-workers millionaires. She worked only a few more months in the big company before her position was redundant.

Exhausted, she came back to Japan, sequestered in a Tokyo apartment, and lived off her separation package. She rarely touched her computer. Instead, she read books. The paper-and-ink kind. Reading a book of poetry one day, she was filled with wonder how the poet twisted words around themselves, dissolving their meaning before reconstructing them. Such beauty and imagination sparked renewed interest in how it might be possible for computers to replicate that kind of creativity, or even develop an understanding of poetry, but without a brain, without a mind. Could the computer, the program, experience the same joy poetry brought her? Could it create poetry, that is, deeply meaningful poetry? Or could it create an original story from a poem? That would be the ultimate proof of concept. If she could develop such a system ... her excitement grew.

She finally got back on her computer. After a day or two reacquainting herself with applicable machine learning algorithms and searching through current research online, she realized implementing her ideas in code was going to be a complex problem. Others tried with mediocre successes, or outright failures.

Her previous experience with machine-generated news stories from a large dataset of newspaper articles was a good place to start. She would need time and resources; in short, a solid job where she could tap into a deep infrastructure. Build a team. Write lots of code. Test prototypes.

She found the opening at ReMoTe, and was hired almost immediately. She helped them invest in powerful servers and cluster them into a super-computer named MountainView after the California town where she last lived. The hardware in place, she brought together her small team to design prototype AI derivatives of their software. They put together a presentation and then went out calling on companies. So far, they hadn't been able to land a client. In her scant free time, she was also able to run her own research project on MountainView. Her research project, never far from her conscious thoughts was one last thread she plucked before the pitch.

Delete thread

With those threads banished, Gina refocused on the presentation for AdCon. She and her team prepared slick slides advocating machine learning text analysis to replace AdCon's survey-based approach to advertising consolidation. A perfect fit, she believed. The key would be to make the proposal understandable and show the improved efficiency and accuracy over AdCon's current approach.

At exactly the scheduled time for the meeting, an AdCon employee escorted them into the conference room where she saw four AdCon wonks and, she presumed, their boss, a middle-aged man who introduced himself but not the others. All five looked tired. Or bored. Probably both. The manager and the four employees wore identical dark-blue blazers, each with a company pin fastened on the left lapel. Some kind of a crazy retro professional look.

While Tokunaga set up their slide deck on the AV computer, Gina introduced herself and her team members, who were not wearing matching blazers, but perhaps they should have been. Gina readied the slide deck, luckily without a hitch, and began. After seeing many pitches in California, her presentation style captured that enthusiastic, but casualness she was used to witnessing. More like a personal conversation.

As she watched the AdCon employees while presenting, conversing, she couldn't tell if they were swayed or not. They seemed to be listening, although perhaps only politely so. She finished and, unlike after a California presentation, bowed formally.

"Thank you very much for your time," Gina said. "We would be happy to answer any questions you might have."

The manager looked to the others at the table. They said nothing. Gina grew a little worried, then realized they were deferring the first question to the manager. Indeed, he asked, "We've heard similar presentations from other AI-focused software companies, so what makes your proposal any different?"

Gina had anticipated that question. "I can't say exactly as I didn't hear their presentations, but I believe what we offer goes beyond what other companies can do. First, we are steeped in the tradition of software development. In other words, a highly iterative approach involving detailed user case analyses, agile prototype development, and rigorous testing. We develop and apply our intelligent algorithms only within that cycle."

She paused for emphasis before she added: "We are not hackers."

The manager folded his arms. "I see. We do have our own research and development team." He nodded at the four others, who must be the R&D team. "How would you work with them?"

"We'd work very closely with your team," she answered while nodding at Tokunaga and Morita. She raised her eyebrows a bit, hoping they would understand the gesture: Please tell them what you do and how you would work with them.

Tokunaga grasped what she wanted. "We're team players, yes, for sure, absolutely. I, for one, played high school baseball so I understand what it means to be on a team, even though our high school team was not very good."

He laughed. Too loudly.

The AdCon team members raised their heads and eyed him with bewilderment. At least he got their attention.

Gina held back a grimace.

Covering for Tokunaga's laugh, Morita spoke up. "From a data perspective, or rather, my perspective as a data engineer, working with your team would be critical. We can't develop the proper data structures without close cooperation from those who know your current data and how you handle that data within established frameworks. For example, do you use a normalized relational database?"

Gina jumped in before Morita could go further. "We understand you have your own research and development team, but what we offer is not an overlap of your efforts. We propose to extend those efforts with more precise predictive analytics. That is, more bang for your buck, as they say."

The manager nodded, then eyed his watch. "Well, we have another meeting. Thank you for your presentation."

Gina thanked them for their time, and offered to answer any questions they might have later. She and her team stood up and bowed in unison.

Instead of going back to the office, Gina treated them to an early dinner at an upscale steak house, chosen despite her vegetarianism. With lite jazz playing in the background, Tokunaga raised his glass of Suntory whiskey with its single cube of gourmet ice. "Cheers to our team."

Morita and Gina raised their glasses. "Cheers."

Gina sipped from her martini glass. "Thank you both for your strong effort."

Morita smacked his lips. "It went well, didn't it?"

Tokunaga nodded. "Very well, I thought. And you, Ono-san?"

Gina smiled broadly. "Yes, excellent. As well as any presentation in Silicon Valley."

"Wow!" said Tokunaga.

They drank heartily to Gina's praise.

Their meals arrived and they dove in. When they were nearly finished, Gina's phone vibrated. She excused herself and took her phone into the restroom. In a stall, she read the text message from the manager at AdCon. He thanked her again for the presentation, then declined their proposal.

"Fuck."

Gina texted back, thanking him for the opportunity to present.

Before returning to the table, she stopped at the bar and ordered another round of drinks. Announcing the rejection could wait until tomorrow. Why spoil the party?

Back in her apartment after the dinner and a post-dinner drinking session with Tokunaga and Morita, Gina changed into her Stanford Athletic Department T-shirt and sweat pants. Not ready to sleep but foggy from the alcohol, she brewed a cup of Kona coffee. The expensive Hawaiian coffee was one of the preferences she developed while in California, a few others being veggie tacos, craft-brewed beer, casual work dress, and the delight-fully useful swear word "fuck."

Sipping the coffee, she sat in front of her computer, opened the slide deck, and considered reasons why the AdCon presentation failed. Nothing seemed immediately obvious. She wondered if the manager would mind a call or email asking for more details about the rejection. Probably a waste of time; he didn't seem to be forthcoming. Besides, she believed they'd already decided they weren't going to hire ReMoTe no matter how well the presentation went. The evidence pointing to that likelihood included the lack of introductions, their perfunctory follow-up questions, even the old-fashioned uniformity of their clothing.

Regardless of the reason, Gina began a self-assessment. Without ques-tion she was disappointed with the rejection for herself, but more for her team and ultimately for ReMoTe. The only way to blunt the announcement was to find something constructive to say about it, especially to her boss, Two-san. She cringed at a mental image of his silent and expressionless, yet penetrating and profound disappointment.

She needed something constructive to hang onto as she rolled down the craggy hill of disappointment. Immediately coming to mind, the intro-duction to ReMoTe rambled too long and dwelled on past accomplish-ments. A list of past clients would have mattered little to a potential client, unless there was a big name or two. She opened a doc and typed:

Skip intro, skip the back story, get right to it.

But what was "it"?

She sulked into the kitchen, opened the fridge, found nothing worthy of the calories. Whenever she needed to think, she paced, or performed a menial task like vacuuming or washing clothes. Neither of those needed doing right now. Walking over to the window, she gazed at the lit-up sky-line. Tokyo was impressive in many ways, but especially at night. Yet with the light show came a wave of loneliness.

Anyway, if the intro slides were the back story, then "it" was the story. The story was the guts of the presentation. The story should have been how ReMoTe could help AdCon improve its targeted ads, making the link be-tween reader and ad more relevant, and thus more profitable. The presentation should start there. That story should be the presentation. She went back to the computer and typed that on the doc.

But, in its essence, what is a story?

In her studies of language processing from a computer science perspective, there had been little mention of story processing. Semantics, speech acts, logic truth tables, sentence structure, linguistics, and probabilities of meaning, yes. Bottomline, stories are simply too difficult, too complex, too variable to be programmable. Much of what a reader, or listener or viewer, requires for story comprehension depends on an understanding of the meaning of related and intertwined action, dialogue, behavior, motivation.

On her own time, she'd poked around narrative theory and craft, and learned about classical plots, simplistic storylines like a character wants something, encounters obstacles to be overcome, and finally attains the something. Twists or subplots could be thrown into the mix: the obstacles force the character in a different direction, a new something emerges, the something doesn't turn out to be what the character imagined.

Most importantly, and obtusely, stories have psychological power. People can easily grasp and remember stories, at least more easily than other kinds of information. Stories were universal among cultures. Whether the power of stories was innate or learned wasn't known.

All right. So, what would the story be in the case of AdCon? It had to be more than increasing profits, didn't it? Perhaps that's all it was, really, but then any software company could promise that. It had to be something more.

She didn't know what. But if she could figure out the right story to tell, would it help when she had to explain to her team why they were rejected by AdCon? Could she write that story? Story on top of story? Recursively programmed stories?

She couldn't think any more about it. She went to the sofa with her coffee and opened a book of poetry that was on the side table. It took a few pages for her mind to quiet and fall into the poems. Noticing that when her reading mind got into a rhythm, the words, phrases, and sentences, resonated with each other, creating a continuity. A story. That's really what story is—a resonance.

After gulping the rest of her lukewarm coffee, she jumped from the sofa and went back to her computer. She opened the code file she started weeks ago, the one that would understand poetry (whatever that concretely means), and then be able to create a story (ditto). She hadn't had much time to work on it while she got things up and running at ReMoTe. Mostly, she recycled some of her code from previous projects, patched them together, and named the Frankenstein monster GRAM.

Yes, from PROGRAM.

When GRAM's minimalist interface opened and connected to the server, there was a notification waiting for her. Oddly so, as she hadn't recalled initiating a run. However it started, the run had ended with a strange error code 631. Something about a server port being improperly opened.

Hmm, had someone been poking at GRAM, tiptoeing around the code, and tripped the switch? Gina looked through the log file, but could find no evidence that someone had logged into the server.

Maybe it was a ghost.

Sure, that's what it was, Gina laughed to herself. A ghost in the machine. Or *deus ex machina*?

She must have left the program running, which it did dutifully until it stopped. A bug might be responsible for opening the port. Well, as long as GRAM had made a training run, she might as well check the results and try a test. From a book of Japanese poetry, she chose an old poem by the poet Ariwara no Narihira.

> This is not the moon,
> nor is this the spring
> of other springs,
> and I alone
> am still the same.

Gina initiated the story creation function. While it ran she fixed another cup of Kona coffee.

She'd sipped about half the cup and read a few more poems before GRAM's story popped up in the results pane.

> I'm lonely and unchanged. I don't know the season. I
> don't know the month.

Hmm ... not very encouraging. GRAM clearly needed something else to improve. For starters more poems. A lot more. She did an online search for poetry databases noting likely ones, especially one housed at the Tokyo Society of Poetry and Poets, until the coffee wore off and she went to bed.

I'm lonely ...

Despite only a couple of hours of sleep, Gina looked more rested than Tokunaga or Morita. Both had pale, blotchy faces and heavy, puffed eyelids. They must have continued drinking, probably at a late-night karaoke bar.

They looked up from their screens but didn't brighten much when Gina set her bag on her desk.

"Good morning," she said with shared weariness.

"Good morning," they answered with raspy voices.

"Shall we have a meeting?"

Both groaned, but pushed themselves away from their desks like overstuffed old men from the dinner table. They trudged behind Gina to a conference room. They plopped into chairs while Gina closed the door.

"Tell us it's good news," said Tokunaga.

Gina sat down. There was no comforting way to put it. "I'm afraid it's not."

Tokunaga bent forward, cradling his head. Morita did the opposite, flinging himself back in the chair as if shot in the face.

When they recovered from the shock, Tokunaga asked her, "What did they say? Was it because of Morita's lack of team spirit?"

"What?" Morita exclaimed wide-eyed. "More likely it was your irrelevant baseball talk."

"It's not just—"

Gina cut short their argument. "They didn't say why they didn't want to hire us. I believe they had, in fact, already made up their minds before we presented. But, looking back at the presentation to find where we could improve, I found that it lacked a story, or rather lacked story."

Morita said, "I don't see the difference."

Tokunaga sulked, "But I did tell a story, remember? About my high school baseball team?"

Morita shook his head. "I don't think that's what she means."

Gina waited to see if they had anything else to put forth before she said, "The story I'm thinking of would have engaged the AdCon team in imagining us working with them, making their work easier, or more productive. That they would receive accolades from their supervisors. They would get promotions, bigger bonuses."

"Unlike us," Morita said.

Tokunaga said, "I thought we gave a good presentation. All those things they could have inferred from what we could do for them."

Gina said, "Perhaps so. But the story needs to be the presentation, rather than leaving it to chance they would infer it."

Tokunaga slapped his palm on the table. "Like starting with the team winning the baseball playoffs."

"There we go with baseball again," said Morita.

"Something like that," Gina said, nodding to Tokunaga.

Morita said, "Come on, facts are better than a story. And I didn't get much of a chance to tell them about our superior data analytics processes. Anyway, it doesn't matter now, we didn't get the contract. What are we going to tell Two-san?"

"Tell him a story!" said Tokunaga.

They laughed a clipped chuckle or two.

"I don't know yet," Gina said. "Overall, I think we need to come up with a better presentation. Call it a story, or whatever. And I have an idea for a potential client that might respond to such a style."

Both of them brightened. "Who?" they asked at the same time.

"I shouldn't say. It's very preliminary. Well, even before preliminary. I need to do more research."

Morita said, "But, I ask again, what do we tell Two-san?"

Gina said, "I'll think of something."

"It better be good," Morita said.

"Hit one out of the park, Ono-san!" Tokunaga swung an imaginary baseball bat.

With her resignation letter neatly folded and tucked in her notebook, Gina made her way to President Taniguchi's office. He'd been with the company from the beginning, rising to senior vice president. He was Employee Number 2, hence his nickname, Two-san. Even when he became president after the founder's death he wanted to remain known as Two-san.

As she neared his office, her thoughts again churned and tangled. The admission of failure wasn't going to be a pleasant conversation, even though Two-san wasn't going to be angry. He'd put a lot of resources and faith in hiring Gina. Of course, she'd gone all in for her own career. She also bore responsibility for Tokunaga and Morita—they'd invested their share of time and energy, possibly at the expense of their jobs.

And she better get going. She lightly rapped a knuckle on his open door.

"Come in," said Two-san.

His shock of white hair always caught her attention. They sat on chairs positioned at ninety-degrees in front of a low table. The angle reduced any full-on face-to-face exchanges, at least not without effort. There was tea, which they sipped. The tea perked her up, as she was still dragging after her caffeine-fueled, sleepless night.

Other than Two-san's hair, her attention was always captured by a photo of Mt. Fuji, its white-capped peak rising above a sea of clouds. Every time she saw the photo, she considered telling him about a distant relative of hers—a not well-known Edo-period woodblock print artist who painted Mt. Fuji everyday for a year, losing his mind in the process, according to family legend. That last fact stopped her from telling Two-san about her ancestor.

"I assume you've been appraised about the AdCon proposal." A pursed-lipped, hopeful smile broke-up his otherwise blank expression.

"Yes. Unfortunately, they declined. The team and I are evaluating our presentation. Not to make excuses, but it seemed that they had already made up their minds and were merely giving us a professional courtesy interview. But again, not to make excuses, we shall always strive to do our best, no matter the circumstances."

She gave Two-san a slow, apologetic, seated bow.

He waved away her gesture.

Gina thought his wave to be pro-forma, as he really did want her to bow. "They might well have had another company in mind. But as we're in rough waters, it's a disappointing result."

His words were heavy with their own gravity. There was nothing Gina could say either way. She waited for the consequences of his disappointment. Was he working up to terminating her employment? She decided she would hand him her letter first, sparing him the indignity.

Two-san sat very still, not focusing on anything, the sad dog look making its appearance. Was he breathing? Maybe he was having a heart attack, following in the footsteps of the company's late founder. Gina cleared her throat. Two-san blinked.

Seeing life, Gina risked telling him about her new project. "I do have an idea to put forth. I've been working on a prototype program on my own time. It analyzes poetry for the underlying story."

"Poetry?"

Speaking with confident enthusiasm, Gina said, "It's a spinoff from my previous work in text analysis used to create news stories."

"Poetry?" Two-san asked again. "You mean Western poetry, or Japanese poetry? Haiku? Renga? I don't see how a poet would be interested in a machine learning program."

"I'm just starting to consider possible use cases," Gina quickly responded, "but right now I'm starting with Japanese poetry. First I need a large database of poetry. Once I have that, I can train the system."

Two-san nodded a couple of times. "I understand the basic idea. However, achieving the end result, a comprehensible story, seems improbable. Poetry is all about complex, subtle nuances, correct? Let me be blunt, poetry is often difficult to understand by people, let alone a machine."

"Absolutely right," Gina said. She thought about announcing her idea of resonance, but decided it was too early, the idea too amorphous. "It's not a trivial programming task. But that makes it all the more compelling to try."

Two-san thought for a moment. "I suppose. But to come back to the main problem, I don't see how it would result in a financially viable contract. Simply put, poetry doesn't engender much capital."

"Agreed. What I might propose is that a sophisticated system like this would demonstrate our expertise. Applications and clients might come along that we haven't yet imagined."

"Interesting proposal," Two-san admitted. "I suppose we could see where this might go, but we still need to pursue more traditional clients and projects."

"Yes, of course," Gina said with all the seriousness she could muster. She started to rise, her resignation letter safe from the light of day.

"Needless to say," Two-san said, not letting hers be the last word, "we don't have all the time in the world."

While leaving Two-san's office, she glanced at the photograph of Mt. Fuji. The mountain seemed different, as if it were now showing a different side. A different view.

There needed to be something else besides the data, something besides the machine learning procedures, to pump up GRAM's literary chops. Gina checked the time. It was still early in the evening. She found her phone and dialed a number. It rang a few times before it clicked, then connected. Instead of a greeting, there was fuzzy silence.

Gina spoke into the fuzziness, "Hello? Mom?"

"Hello?" said her mother in a soft distant voice.

"Mom, it's me Gina. Turn your phone around."

The sound of fumbling was followed by, "Gina?"

"Yes, who else?"

Gina didn't expect her mother, Kumi Ono, to help with the poetry-story project, even though she was an early artificial intelligence programmer. It wasn't because she'd retired, or rather hadn't worked in the business after her father's business, Ono Robotics, folded over twenty years ago. It wasn't because her mother's expertise was ancient AI, learned before there were breakthroughs in hardware especially faster chips and new algorithms and machine learning. Nor was it because her mother was an alumna of UC Berkeley, Stanford's rival. No, it was because her mother lived in a world that Gina found unfathomable.

"Yes, who else?" her mother repeated after fumbling with the phone.

"How are you?" Gina asked.

Again repeating her daughter, Kumi said, "How are you?"

"I'm fine, thank you."

"Fine, thank you."

"Good," said Gina, then added quickly before her mother could repeat, "I'm working on a new artificial intelligence project and I'm kind of stuck. The idea is to take poetry, a set of poems, and create a story after entering a poem. I'm using machine learning of course but so far the results are lacking in, well, I guess, I'd call it story-ness."

"Hmm," came out of the phone. The sound was her mother's usual response when she couldn't repeat a longer string of words. Or when she hadn't been paying attention. At least that's what Gina believed.

"Of course," Gina continued, "there are the standard hard problems of natural language processing, common sense understanding of the world, genuine affective reactions, and others. But I feel there must be a place to start. I don't know exactly what I'm asking, but I thought you might have an idea."

There was a lengthy silence before her mother pronounced in a voice barely above a whisper, "Evidence of sexual attraction itself will offer a clue to aesthetic rules."

Now Gina was silent, taking in what Kumi said, not grasping the meaning. She typed the declaration into a notepad. Before Gina could ask her to elaborate, her mother disconnected.

Gina stared at the silent phone for a moment, then re-read her mother's words. She read them several times before shutting down her computer for the night.

A Few Years Ago

"By a vote of sixteen to one, Yurika Hamada is removed from the board of the Japan Poetry Congress. Meeting adjourned."

After making his pronouncement, Congress President Saito exited the dais so quickly a few strands of his slicked-back hair came unglued. The rest of the board members followed him with the same sense of haste, only a couple of them dawdling as if to give Yurika a mouthed "sorry" in condolence, thoughts swiftly dismissed as they realized the gestures would be obvious in their insincerity given the all-but unanimous vote.

The sole opposition vote was, of course, Yurika's.

The rest of the Congress, those members in the audience numbering nearly sixty, drifted out in clumps, silently or with trailing whispers, until the only ones left were two men sitting together in the back row. Yurika didn't immediately recognize them, and they too left before she could recall who they were.

Saito's final words evaporated, leaving a vacuous silence that gave her a shiver of dread. Yurika wondered why the words struck her like such a matter of life and death. Words, language, that's all we really have to our claim of humanity. Yet, while some words were bright, sharp with precise meaning, others were dull with vagueness. For one, "removed," as in "removed from the board." More like "kicked off." Or metaphorically "assassinated." Colloquially, "shown the exit," although not literally as she was now the only person in the room.

Japanese words were particularly problematic, one reason being the differences between the *kun'yomi* and *on'yomi* reading of Japanese written characters imported from China. For example, the character for "water" has a kun'yomi word of Japanese origin and an on'yomi word of Chinese origin. In terms of poetics, the difference between the two readings, even while both signify the same thing—water—can be laden with multiple, sometimes highly divergent meanings. The Japanese kun'yomi reading is suffused with the Shinto reverence for the purifying power of water. While the Chinese reading, the on'yomi, refers to the prosaic substance of the liquid. It's even more complicated than that, and the subtle, ticklish nature of the differences can be lost on even the best poets.

But that sub-theory of poetics wasn't why she was voted off the board, voted out of the Congress really—why would she want to remain a member after such a public humiliation? No, the reason was there, on the dais, on her copy of the meeting agenda. As usual, she'd annotated the agenda in her precise handwriting during the discussion of each item. For one, next to "Session proposals for the annual conference" she'd noted: "Again, my proposal for presenting the origins and influence of the Dark Ravine poetry strain was denied ... for lack of interest?!"

Scanning down to the last item on her last agenda, her notes became furious scrawls:

> S_ says "pure supposition, zero evidence"
> B_ "a minor poet from a minor school"
> K_ "not worthy of another moment of our time"
> S_ "probably not even a real person"
> A_ "if Hamada-san remains intractable ... well, her presence on the board is no longer tenable"

There's another word, "intractable," with a rich stew of divergent meanings. "Out-of-control," "unmanageable," or the worst one of all, "burdensome." Who wants to be a burden? Yet, when one is in the right and simply pointing out that fact, or even if there's a strong possibility of being right, and requesting further discussion, the situation might be considered a burden, but certainly not the person.

At the end of that mental reinforcement, the lights in the room went out, one row at a time. She hadn't noticed anyone entering the room to flick the switches. Mostly likely the lights were auto-controlled by movement sensors. She'd been sitting so still, frozen, the sensors assuming no life remained.

Yet somewhere in the dark, a plan was beginning to flourish.

3

High Noon

At high noon, the sun did its best to pierce the dense forest, peeking into the narrow cleft of the dark ravine before vanishing.

Thinking back on it, Akikaze was surprised he found the small shrine at all. One would have to trip over it to find it. Why would a shrine be built in a place that was so dark? Although, perhaps it was because of the darkness that the shrine existed in its location—as solace to the people who lived nearby, wherever that was. Akikaze hadn't heard of any village in this area. But then he also hadn't anticipated being chased down an animal path into the ravine by a pervert-hating farmer wielding a scythe.

Now warmed and dry, and having avoided disaster with the village woman, he left the shrine to search for the priest, hoping to find him alive and well if likely a little battered from the fall. He also hoped the farmer returned to his harvest, so Akikaze could retrieve his bag. It would be good fortune if both happened so he could be on his way, wandering.

It took him a while to find the path he used earlier. He couldn't remember exactly which direction he came from, and it was, after all, a tiny, narrow path. But he did and was able to trace his steps back up the ridge. He thought about calling out for the priest but was worried the farmer might be on the prowl for perverts. That thought made him look around for another stick he could use as a club, but remembering his previous misadventure, he went on without a weapon.

When he came to the spot where he had climbed down to the stream, he stopped and focused down into

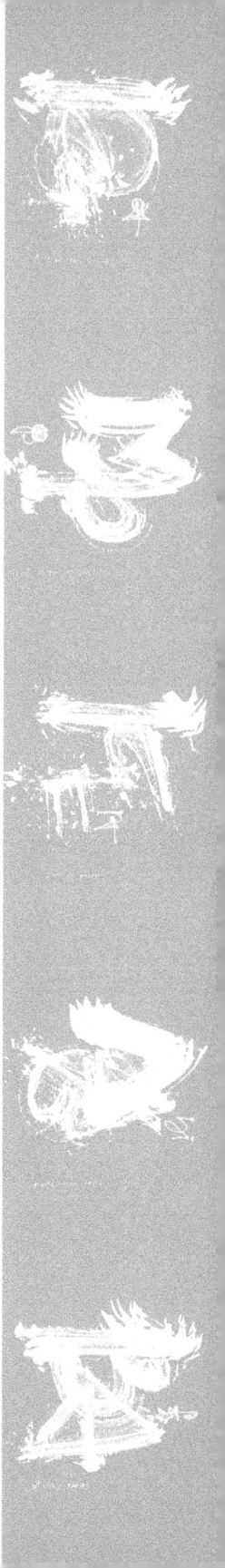

Hello again.

     Hi.

The story, S, includes a running imagery of darkness. Even at high noon, the sun appears only for a blink of an eye. This imagery provides background mood, a literary device that creates, or provokes, a feeling in the reader, R. There can be other factors, perhaps many, that contribute to mood.

In fact, everything in the story conceivably contributes to mood. In this case, the setting of the story—the ravine—creates the darkness, which in turn creates, or adds to, the mood, M.

Symbolically, this could be $M = L + C + V$ [Where M is mood, which is the sum of other variables or contributing factors including L (location, or setting), C (character), and V (voice).]

Of course, readers may react to these factors differently, depending on cultural, individual, or other background influences. Also, there are possibly other factors contributing to M which need to be defined or clarified.

     Good, and yes, that makes sense. Back to the story?

Yes!

the depths. There wasn't a priest resting on the banks, recovering from the fall. Nor was there anyone else. He thought about climbing down, wading in the stream. But the thought of the cold water made him shiver. Maybe after he retrieved his bag. So, he kept walking along the path, peering down to the stream where he could.

Despondency bloomed when he considered that he wasn't going to find the priest, alive or not. His wanderings hadn't gone well, but this was the worst. He'd been a student of the poet Zatsuyou after running away from his family business growing mulberry trees and selling the leaves to silk producers to feed their silkworms. No doubt his parents and siblings hadn't noticed he'd been gone for several days; they wouldn't have been concerned until he was due to submit the remissions he collected on his delivery route. Being the fourth child and the third son, he was unremarkably centered in the family's sibling rankings.

His mother would have said, "Where's Third Son? He's late with his payments."

"Go look in the teahouse in town," his father would have answered. "He fancies himself a poet. They gather there."

Akikaze's poetry school ranking was not any higher than his familial ranking, certainly nowhere near stellar. Besides his mediocre talent, there was a strict hierarchical ranking system by seniority, and it would take him ten years to rise to the top of that system. The lower-ranking students received less instruction time, fewer chances to join the linked verse parties, and as in any artistic apprenticeship, he was required to clean the rooms, sweep the garden, and make tea after instruction.

But without complaint, he performed his share of the duties and worked diligently at his poetry. In short, he did all he could to stay at the top of his cohort, while trying to catch the ear, or eye, of Zatsuyou. But the pace was agonizingly slow, and after several years he realized he'd likely go no further. So he struck out on his own. As had been the case with his family, he doubted many would notice his departure, nor would more than a few even care.

Surviving through menial jobs, he struggled to find time to work on his poetry. But little-by-little he managed to fill up the journals he bought with spare coins. Then, one of his bosses found out that Akikaze knew how to keep accounts, as he had done with his family business. The boss offered him a chance to keep accounts for a merchant. That position provided him steady, less demanding work, and he was able to spend more time on his poems.

At a teahouse he frequented, he met a few other poets. They formed a loose, ragged group, without hierarchy, without leaders, and rarely the same members from month to month.

After a few years, he and a small group of the poets set off on a journey following paths of the earlier poets they admired. The journey quickly dissolved into acrimonious disputes on which direction to go, where to stop for the night, when to write or drink. Not to mention that Akikaze was one of the few who had saved funds for the trip.

One-by-one, the traveling poets dropped out until only Akikaze remained. The last one to leave made off with the rest of Akikaze's money. Despite that, Akikaze enjoyed the quiet and solitary time for a while, and his poetry reflected that inner contemplation. He visited a few famous spots, paid homage by writing his reflective versions.

Then he slipped into his own deep, self-reflection, wondering if he would ever write a good, or even decent, poem. He spent days writing, barely eating, barely sleeping. He became ill, found an abandoned shack to recover, barely surviving. Dreams and nightmares mingled with memories and snippets of the light streaming through the cracks in the walls.

When he finally emerged, he began his wandering again, this time truly wandering without purpose or destination. He lived as he could, finding handouts when the hunger drove him into a village, or trading a day of labor for a meal and a straw mat for the night. His poetry wandered as well, delving into the solitude of his journey, the length of a breath of air, the different shades of light or darkness. He realized he left part of his soul in that abandoned shack. But none of the pain prepared him for the farmer and the priest. All he wanted in his life was to get back to the simplicity of wandering.

He made it to the place where he struck the priest. Akikaze's bag was under the deformed tree, a relief of sorts. Picking up the bag, the weight comforting, he walked over to the edge of the path. Peering down the steep slope, to the bottom of the cliff, he saw no sign of the priest.

He headed back down the path toward the shrine. On the way, he kept an eye down into ravine, and occasionally called out to the priest. But there was nothing, no sighting, no response.

Finally, back at the shrine, exhausted from the trip, he went in, hoping the priest would be back there, recovering from his fall.

"There you are," said a voice.

Akikaze discretely placed his bag in a corner of shrine. A smell of salty broth mingled with the lingering scent of incense.

"You must be feeling better," said the mushroom soup woman from the shadows. "You went out."

"Just briefly. I needed to collect something."

"I could have done that for you," she said quietly. "But never mind. I brought your soup. Please wash up and I'll serve it."

"Thank you, but I wouldn't want you to spend more time on me. I'm sure I can serve myself."

After a lengthy moment of silence, she turned without a word and went toward the back of the shrine. Apparently his protestation was rejected. Akikaze waited for another moment or two then followed her. He found her carrying a pot from the kitchen to the small adjacent room where there was a low table.

He stopped to rinse his hands in a bowl of water, then went into the room and knelt to tuck his legs under the table. She ladled soup in a bowl.

"It smells wonderful," he said.

"It's just mushroom soup," she said.

Akikaze almost said, "To a wandering poet it's a feast." Instead, he murmured his appreciation.

She moved close to him while ladling the soup. Out of the corner of his eye, he thought she was looking at him with a soft, intelligent expression. He wondered if she'd ever been this close to the priest. Likely not, although there was some level of comfort between the two of them, hence her light scolding.

When she finished filling his bowl, she scooted over to the side of the room, likely waiting for him to try the soup. He started to pick up the bowl but then put it down. She was waiting for him to say a prayer.

After a quick, common prayer, Akikaze took a loud, wet, appreciative sip.

"Delicious," he said.

She gave him a quick bow of her head. "It's merely the poor village meal you've had ten thousand times."

He took another loud sip to show his pleasure, despite having eaten it, apparently, ten thousand times. That number, even if an exaggeration, told him the priest had been in the village a long time. So Akikaze being mistaken for the priest wasn't because the priest had been recently installed.

Actually, it was very good soup. He took another noisy sip.

The mushroom soup woman said, "It's so dark in here. Shall I light the lamp?"

A drop of soup caught in his throat as he swallowed the "No!" he wanted to shout. "Thank you, but no." He added hastily, "I'm used to the dark."

The woman made another of her murmurs, the tone of which implied she thought he was out of my mind to be used to this much darkness, but she would let him have his way.

After another few sips of soup, she said, "Thank you again for your prayer for my husband. I'm still thinking about it."

"You're welcome," said Akikaze. "I didn't realize I was saying anything too different from the, my, usual prayer."

"If I can be blunt, usually you quickly say the same prayer. I appreciate that you pray for him, for us, so I'm not complaining. Not at all. It's just that, well, I liked the new prayer. It seemed more sincere."

She bowed her head again.

The poet didn't know what to say, especially worried anything he said would change her perception of him. He could tell her the truth, but no telling how that would be taken. Not well, likely.

He finished his soup. The woman shuffled over to the table. "Would you like some more?"

"No, I'm satisfied."

"Satisfied," she repeated as if it were the first time she'd heard the word. "I'll leave the pot if you want more later."

"Excellent."

"You seem to be feeling better."

"Yes, I am. The soup did the trick. And your presence."

She made her murmuring sound again. "Oh!"

Wondering where the mushroom soup woman lived, how she survived in the dark ravine, but being unable to ask her things which he, that is, the priest, should already know—Akikaze retraced the woman's steps out of the shrine. Taking the main path, assuming it would be the route she would have taken, he walked carefully to avoid tripping in the dark or making too much noise in case a villager happened to be nearby.

The path was wider, less rough than the animal track he took along the ridge, so he was able to walk with more confidence. He wasn't sure, however, what he was going to do when he encountered villagers, or especially if he managed to find the woman. On one hand if the woman hadn't noticed he wasn't the priest, then others might find him unrecognizable as well. On the other hand the woman may not have ever been in as close contact with the priest as others. Although she did say his voice was different, if only slightly.

But that left the question, why was he able to pass for the priest at all, at least with the woman? Was there a physical resemblance? In the brief encounter with the priest, Akikaze wouldn't have said there was considerable resemblance. It wasn't as if he had unexpectedly encountered his twin brother, or as if he were seeing himself in a mirror for the first time.

Akikaze believed he had unremarkable features, although we look different to others than to ourselves. And the poet hadn't seen himself in a mirror for a long time. How long, he couldn't remember. His traveling life no doubt had changed his appearance. He touched his face, felt its gaunt, etched cheekbones and sunken cheeks.

He heard a voice, then another. They were men's voices, too far for him to make out what they were saying. Then the voices faded. The men were going in the same direction as he was, so he continued his trek.

After walking a long while, more than two thousand steps (he was in the habit of counting them on his journey), he spotted a small building not far ahead. The light from a lamp illuminated some of the building, likely a house, although it was more of a hut than anything more substantial. Akikaze felt a poem coming forth, capturing the lone hut in a dark ravine, a stream of weak light barely spilling out.

Dusk was approaching, but, of course, it was already dark in the ravine. He stopped when he saw a movement inside the hut. He stepped off the path and skirted around the outside, trying to see inside. There was a wisp of smoke in the back. Getting closer, he recognized a simple brazier used for making charcoal. From his experience, it was an inefficient way to make a lot of charcoal. Maybe there wasn't much need for it.

Walking past, he kept an eye open for any of the occupants. No one came out. He returned to the path. He walked a little further until he came to a cluster of buildings, slightly larger than the hut. Maybe a dozen in total, half on one side of the path, and half on the other. The buildings weren't all of the same size—some more like the hut he first encountered, some larger and more elaborate, with verandas, for instance. Oddly, not only were there differences in size and style, they were also scattered in their location, as if the builders paid no attention to the other structures when they laid out the foundations.

Two men, possibly the ones he heard earlier, were walking into one of the larger buildings which was more-or-less centered in the mix. Other voices came from the larger building after the men entered.

Akikaze backed away from the path while keeping an eye out for other residents of the village. Coming to the edge of the surrounding forest, he found a hidden spot where he could watch the village and its occupants. From his vantage point, the haphazard placement of the buildings seemed even more severe.

After a short while, a man and a woman came out of one the smaller homes. The woman carried a package, or maybe a bowl or pot wrapped in cloth—it was difficult to see much in the darkness. They also entered the larger building.

Soon after the couple disappeared, a man and woman along with two children came out of another house. The parents each carried a wrapped bowl. They entered the larger building and the voices from inside grew louder.

There must be a communal meal this evening, Akikaze mused. Why hadn't he—the priest—been invited? Perhaps the priest didn't participate in the lives of the villagers outside of the shrine.

While he was contemplating that, a woman came out of the third house closest to him. He was sure, even in the dark, that she was the woman from the shrine. Walking quickly over to the large building, she carried a pot, probably her contribution to the dinner. Mushroom soup?

After she entered, Akikaze waited a while to make sure that she wasn't just delivering some food. When she didn't reappear, he edged around the forest until he was close to her home. Pausing, he saw no one else making their way over to the communal building, so he hurried across the cleared space and to the back of the house. Carefully stepping on the small veranda, he listened for anyone still inside. Having heard nothing, he tried the sliding panel door. It opened easily and he stepped inside.

The home was neither one of the smaller ones, nor one of the larger. It seemed to be one room, with two screens that partitioned it into smaller spaces. One of the rooms along the perimeter had racks of wood, on which were a few drying mushrooms. The earthy, woody smell was intense. He wondered how they made a living from the meager crop that would come out of the drying room. In the middle of the room there was a cooking hearth, and near its warmth, there was a lingering aroma of her mushroom soup.

Continuing in further, he found no one else. The household must just be the woman and her husband, no children, no parents. As was the shrine, the home was well-worn in places where footsteps were frequently taken, or touched by hands. And like the shrine, it was clean and comfortable. The furnishings were sparse as well—a low table, a small cabinet where the bedding was stored, and another cabinet with clothing. There was a chest where dishes and other household items were stored.

Akikaze opened the clothes cabinet even as he felt he was now becoming the pervert the rice farmer had accused him of being. Unable to resist, he slid his fingertips over a garment of hers, the soft fabric as pleasant to the touch as was the smell of her coming from the cabinet.

Outside, the wind picked up—the fresh, cool air drifted inside through slivers of openings in the walls of the old, rickety home. The wind drove him outside and back to the edge of the forest. He crossed the path and walked around the other side of the clearing in the forest until he was across from the larger building.

He could see shadowed movement inside. Taking a chance, he stole across the clearing to the building. Holding his breath, he peered into a sliding panel that was partially open.

Ten or so people were sitting at long table, busily sharing a meal. There was an older man, with white, bushy hair, seated at the head of the table. Occasionally there was a compliment on the food, some laughing to a response, but little conversation. Nothing that would give him more knowledge of the village, its people, its place on the world.

For that matter, what might he say about his place in the world?

The woman from the shrine was seated so he could see her right pro-file. She spoke only a word or two, here and there. It was as if she were thinking about something besides the meal or the conversation.

Then, she turned and looked straight toward him.

4

His Shy Smile

The Tokyo Society of Poetry and Poets was headquartered in a chaotic neighborhood of narrow alleys full of tiny bars and restaurants, used bookstores, vinyl record shops, and who knew what else. The Society itself was in a modern, bunker-style concrete building, its rough, gray rawness softened with randomly-placed planters of bamboo.

Gina pulled on the brass door handle, green with patina except where fingers wore it away. The lobby was a large open space furnished with only a simple desk of metal and trimmed with bamboo at which was seated a receptionist.

"Good afternoon," Gina said.

"Good afternoon," replied the receptionist. His longish hair was cut in a simple, angular style that complimented the building's architecture. "How may I help you?"

"I'm here for a meeting with Kenzo Karaki."

The receptionist focused at a space in front of him, then poked at the air. After a moment he announced, "Your three o'clock appointment is here."

"Okay," answered a disembodied voice.

Wow. A holographic screen. A virtual intercom.

The receptionist again poked at the invisible screen. "Karaki-san will be with you shortly. Would you care for a cup of tea?"

Gina didn't see a tea service. Curious how the receptionist might conjure up a cup of tea, Gina said that she would like one and thanked him.

"You're welcome."

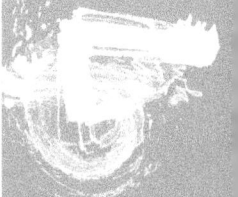

The receptionist placed a fingertip on the invisible screen. He got up and walked over to a section of wall, waited a few moments, then reached out his hand, seemingly through the wall. In his hand was a cup, a cloud of steam rising from it.

He brought it to Gina. "Impressive technology," Gina said.

The receptionist, however, seemed unimpressed with the invisible tea service nor with Gina's appreciation of it. Gina took a sip of the tea—perfect in flavor and temperature.

"Excellent. Thank you."

The receptionist nodded and went back to his desk to work on his invisible computer.

Such high-tech wasn't what Gina had expected when she called the Society to inquire about their database she'd selected from her search. What had she expected? An older building, with shelves overflowing with books. A row of older computers for making searches. A smell of moldering paper and ink.

A man appeared seemingly out of nowhere, as if he walked through the wall. The wizardry didn't want to end.

"Hello," the man said as he approached. Tall, about her age, his hair was also longish although non-styled, towel-combed with some of the hairs cascading over his forehead in wavy bangs, spilling onto his glasses.

Gina answered, "Hello." She stood up.

"I'm Kenzo Karaki," he said.

"Gina Ono. Thank you for meeting me with such short notice."

"You're welcome. It's not a problem.This way."

As they walked toward the section of wall from which he'd appeared, Gina said, "You have incredible technology."

He laughed a little. "One of our late benefactors bequeathed us funds to experiment with the latest tech. But you're here on a good day. It tends to crash with some regularity."

"That's too bad," said Gina. "It looks like fun."

"Watch this," he said.

When they reached the wall, Gina could see a shimmering in the otherwise solid work panel. Without hesitation, Kenzo Karaki walked into the simmering. After a brief hesitation, Gina followed him.

On the other side, she said, "Cool."

There was a corridor leading to a warren of office spaces on one side, and a large open space of bookshelves on the other. More like what she originally expected for a poetry society.

"This is the staff area," said Kenzo. "We also have the library, study rooms, public reading rooms, the archives. I'll give you a tour later, if you'd like."

"Yes, I'd like that."

He turned to look at her as if to judge the veracity of her response. He gave her a nod, then stopped at an office door. Gina went in first. There was a small round table at which they sat. Gina placed her teacup and bag on the table. "Thank you again for seeing me so quickly."

"You're welcome. So, what can I do for you? Specifically, that is. I know you are interested in our digital archives from your message."

Tell the story, Gina reminded herself. Leave out the dry facts.

"Imagine you wake up this morning and wonder how the use of a word, say for example 'raincloud,' varies over several poems. Or you might be curious how the meaning of raincloud differs from poet to poet. Perhaps you would like to trace its use over several generations of poets. I imagine something like this might happen fairly often. I don't know exactly how you would begin to research this, but I assume you could run a search through the digital archives you have available. You would have the output of poems that could be further filtered and sorted. Then you could start going through them and coding the instances for whatever parameters or uses or meaning you were interested in. I assume this would take a considerable amount of time."

She took a sip of tea to give him time to respond. So far, he hadn't shown an expression that would give away his level of interest.

He said, "It depends on the complexity for the analysis, but yes, something like that," Then he asked, "Before you go further, who is your favorite poet?"

Gina's mind quickly flipped from the next part of her story to wondering why he asked that question and how she would answer it. Stalling for some time to think, she said, "I have to admit, I'm not the most well-read in poetry, but I do like it and appreciate it."

Then she remembered the recent poem she'd entered into GRAM. "I like Ariwara no Narihira." She repeated as much of the poem as she could remember. Then she mentioned her earlier thoughts of how poets could twist words around themselves, dissolve their meaning before reconstructing them.

The database engineer perked up a little, as if he heard a distant, not unpleasant noise. "I haven't heard it put that way before. Interesting. But sorry to interrupt. You were saying something about your proposed search function?"

She went on: "Now imagine that you came into work, made a cup of tea, set up your analysis of 'raincloud' before lunch, go to lunch, and when you return, you will have your analysis ready to inspect."

He tapped his fingertips together. It was some kind of reaction at least.

Gina suddenly felt as if she were floating, trying to run with no traction. At last she found solid ground: "But not only is the search analysis complete, but a story has been told."

The archivist brushed the hair away from his glasses. He stared at Gina with a hard, penetrating gaze.

Then he smiled. It was a funny looking smile, kind of crooked, kind of shy. But nonetheless, it was a smile.

Had she deviated from the story and delved into dry facts? Gina thought how she might get her presentation, informal as it was, back on track.

Before she could start again, his shy smile vanished as quickly as it appeared, a short-lived bubble floating in the air, bright and shiny in the sun, pricked by a shard of wind. He said, "Please, go ahead. I'm interested."

"Do you have any questions so far?"

"I have many questions, but perhaps you will answer them before I need to ask."

Thoughtful of him. Gina said, "Thank you. As I was saying, I'm not a poet, not even much of a poetry reader. I'm more of a science fiction fan. Say, is there any science fiction poetry?"

"Hmm, I don't know of any off the top of my head. I can't imagine there isn't any at all. I'll have to do some research."

Gina straightened up in her chair. "Thanks, it was just an impulsive thought. Back to what I was saying, again, about 'story' ... it's more than merely an analysis, there's a story created from the analysis."

She told him about her evening reading poetry, how just examining the words and their literal meaning would not have produced the resonance she felt with the poems. "The resonance created the feeling of a story, getting lost in a different word, in other people's lives."

Kenzo looked to the side, then tilted his head. "I'm an archives database engineer so I can only assume the best poetry does this. Unfortunately, I don't believe many people get to your level of appreciation. Most readers don't let the words create the story, or the resonance of a story as you say. I think they try to force their own narrative onto the words. Conversely, experts are counting syllables or discerning rhythm and structure."

He paused, letting his words sink in. "But you have something else to say about your reason for being here, don't you?"

It was Gina's turn to smile. So far, so good. Now she might get to the facts. "I work for a software development company, Red Moss Technology, heading their artificial intelligence division. I'm also doing my research in this area, in the general area of natural language processing, machines understanding and producing speech and text. It struck me that having machines able to ingest, or read, poetry, and have the same sort of experience as I did, would be the highest level of achievement for computers. Does this make sense?"

Kenzo looked off into the distance. "I have nothing even approaching your level of knowledge in this area. Since I work in the area of digital archives, my technical background is in preservation and data, not artificial intelligence. But I have interest in it and have done some reading. It's my impression that what you are proposing would be ... difficult to say the least. I'm sure there are a lot of details you have considered that are necessary to make it, whatever it is, work as you envision."

"Absolutely correct. The main consideration is one of data, especially in machine learning."

He stopped her. His expression had gone rigid. "I know the basic idea behind machine learning, but don't understand it well enough to be of help."

Gina felt a rising frustration. She had gotten off the story again. "It's your ultimate assistant, one who never sleeps, one who can look for a needle in a Mt. Fuji-sized set of data. It can create classifications, find patterns, and, perhaps, ultimately tell you, and tell the patrons of your Society

Welcome back.

> Thanks.

So, the character's smile is "shy." Another literary device is employed here. The smile is given a human-quality; that is, the actor (the smiler) can be shy, and a particular kind of smile reveals that shyness. But the smile itself is not shy. This literary device is called "anthropomorphism."

Usually this device is more obvious, such as when animals are given human qualities such as the ability to speak. But the point holds here—the smile has a mind of its own.

> Ha.

Symbolically, $C(a) \sim o(a)$ [Where $C(a)$ is a character's attribute, $o(a)$ is an object's attribute, and $\sim$ signifies equivalence.]

> Thank you. That looks good. For now, though, I'm curious why the smile is so shy.

Good! The story, S, continues.

a story."

Kenzo softened. "I certainly can understand that. Let's skip the details for now then. In a general sense, what are you wanting me to do? Can you tell me that?"

"Sure. To get straight to the point, I'd like you to hire us to create this poetry analysis and story creation artificial intelligence program that can do all those things."

Kenzo's face went blank, then his shy smile made another of its brief appearances. "That is straight to the point. I can't imagine us doing that, even though you tell a compelling story. I'm only a mid-level staff person in the technology division, but I doubt the directors in charge of the archives will give anyone such unfettered access to the files. Maybe if you can come up with some other ways we might work together?"

"I can appreciate your reluctance. Perhaps if we took it by smaller steps, say helping with a specific kind of text analysis. Something we might be able to do as a free demonstration for you to see the value of what we are proposing. If you could provide me with a dataset to work with."

"A demo might help, but I can't promise anything. I'd need some specific examples of what the scale of a demonstration project looks like. I wouldn't want to suggest something beyond what you are thinking of, or conversely, not robust enough to fully show us what this means for us."

"Of course. I'll put together some ideas that we can discuss."

"Excellent. Shall we go on that tour I promised? I'll tell you the story of the Society."

Gina laughed.

"Sorry for the brief tour," Kenzo apologized a few minutes later. "Got to run to a meeting."

"It was a nice tour," Gina said.

"A short story."

"Still, nice."

Kenzo left Gina in the lobby with the frowning receptionist who was fiddling with the virtual screen. Glancing up he said, "I hope you had a good visit."

It had been. Kenzo was more receptive than others she's pitched to lately. Doing it one-on-one might have helped. Launching right into a story, too. She hoped he would come through with a juicy poetry dataset.

Kenzo's mini-tour enhanced the visit. As they walked through the building, he told her how the Society had risen from the ashes after the war. They lost some original books and scrolls in the firestorms, but had managed to save the majority by carrying them by the armloads out of the city to safe locations.

Gina told the receptionist she was especially intrigued by the Ancient Archive Room.

The receptionist brightened. "The AAR. Incredible, isn't it! Original poems from hundreds of years ago. Some a thousand years."

"Very cool, for sure." Gina stepped closer to the receptionist's desk. "Can you ... oh, you smell nice."

"Thank you!" he said with a grin. "It's called 'Hand-Sawn Cedar.' Can I ...?"

"Just curious if you can see the AAR from your monitor?"

With a couple of finger jabs in the air, the room appeared on the monitor revealing its humidity-controlled, barely illuminated cases, each holding scrolls or delicate sheets of paper with faded but gorgeous calligraphy.

At home later that evening, and with Two-san's warning to get clients or else still echoing through her mind, Gina worked through a search of possible clients. Not finding any that grabbed her attention, she logged into the MountainView server. As with last time, there was a notification—error 631, port open. She dutifully checked the log and found no reason for the error or the open port. Curious. There must be a way of finding out how it was happening. Or if was happening at all. She could set up a tracer, a couple of lines of code that would trigger when the port was open, or closed for that matter, and save additional information for later.

For now, she wanted to try out GRAM with a prompting poem by Yamabe no Akahito, her selection inspired by the photograph in Two-san's office.

> I passed by the beach
> at Tago and saw
> the snow falling, pure white,
> high on the peak of Fuji.

After starting the story generation function, she wandered over to her window and looked out at the Tokyo skyline. There was no Mt. Fuji in the panorama, but even if it were clear daylight, she didn't think she could see the peak from her location. Maybe though ... she'd check tomorrow. But for now, what did she wish GRAM would do with the poem?

That was a good question. After all, she wasn't a fiction writer. Even after reading fiction, and the little bit of literary theory that she'd studied, she wouldn't by any stretch be anything more than an amateur writer. But she did know better fiction from poorer fiction. Or did she? Maybe she only knew what she liked. That said, or rather, that thought, she tried to create a story using the poem, with its resonance.

She read the poem again. It was kind of a story already, at least there was some action, minimal as it was. The narrator of the poem, the main character, the only character, was walking, then noticed it was snowing at the very top of Mt. Fuji. It was merely an observation rather than a plot.

Actually, there were more questions than plot. Was the character walking? The character could have been sailing past the beach. Or running. Or horseback riding. Why was the character passing the beach? We know nothing, except that the character wasn't so resolute in their travels that they wouldn't notice the snow falling. There was even a casualness to the movement.

About the snow—was there something unusual about it? Its pure whiteness was noted. While snow is always white, at least while it was falling, there could be other shades of white. Blue-white, silver-white. Was the interest in the snow because it was so white, or because it was snowing high up on the peak? Maybe it was an unusual meteorological phenomenon to see it snowing high on the peak.

Yet, even with all the ambiguity, all the questions, there was a resonance of a story. A feeling of ... a life changing event. Yes, that's what she felt. But what's the story that would go along with it?

She turned away from the window and went back to the computer screen. GRAM had come up with its story.

Going somewhere, I walked along the sand near an ocean. I stopped. It was snowing far away.

The banal micro-story made her laugh. But it wasn't entirely horrible either.

Thinking about it more, GRAM hadn't done much more than explain the poem. Not the ultimate goal, that's for sure. More poems in the database would help. She wondered how Kenzo Karaki was faring with his request for the Society to work with her and ReMoTe.

But wait ... she looked up her notes and re-read her mother's cryptic remark: "Evidence of sexual attraction itself will offer a clue to aesthetic rules."

What did it mean, exactly? Why evidence of sexual attraction and not just sexual attraction? Which aesthetic rules? And why only a clue to them? All questions she'd have to ask her mother. Not that she expected a rational answer from her increasingly distant, or just plain weird, mother.

Then, a wild thought: Maybe GRAM would understand what the statement meant, or even better, use it. She re-started the story-generation function, this time appending her mother's statement to the Mt. Fuji poem. After hitting enter, she went to get ready for bed.

When she returned, GRAM was still running. She let it continue, went back to her bedroom, and fell asleep almost as soon as she folded herself onto the bed.

It's snowing, far away on Mt. Fuji. I feel the cold. I hurry on my way to see my lover. Will he be seeing another?

"A demonstration project?" repeated Tokunaga.

"Approved by Two-san?" repeated Morita.

Gina broke the news to them after lunch. They perked up from their post-meal lethargy as she briefed them on her meeting with Two-san and also the Tokyo Society of Poetry and Poets.

"Poetry?" they repeated together.

"Think of it as data. Poetry is just data."

Morita rubbed his forehead. "*Text* data."

"*Text* analysis," moaned Tokunaga.

"True," Gina said in a comforting voice. "Text data and analyses are more challenging than numerical data. But, relax, it's a demo. We can limit the size of the dataset and the complexity of the analysis."

"Will that be enough of a demo to convince the Poetry Society?" asked Tokunaga.

Morita said, "That's a good point. If it's too simple, they may not be impressed."

"I agree," Gina said. "We'll have to get more details from them about possible projects they might find impressive. Morita-san, how much data storage space can we handle?"

"If it's flash storage, then maybe a terabyte. But it's relatively easy to add memory."

"Okay," said Gina. "Tokunaga-san, can we add processing power to the cluster?"

"More than the seven hundred fifty-six gigabytes available? It's not so easy to add RAM. It's easier to add more blades to the cluster. Just let me know what you need, and how I pay for it."

"Understood. Thank you both. I'll get more information to you as soon as possible."

As they were leaving the conference room, Morita asked Gina, "Is this our last chance?"

"Don't worry about that," she answered as confidently as she could.

The Society was just about to close to the public for the day. Gina admired the lobby's high-tech accoutrements as she waited for Kenzo. The receptionist poked in the air, stabbing at the holographic image, while mumbling something.

Gina said, "It's not cooperating?"

Startled, the receptionist jumped a little. "Nope."

"And just when you want to leave."

"Uh huh," he said.

"I work in tech, although I'm not sure I can help you. But what's the problem?"

He stabbed again. "Freezing. It happens a couple of times a day." He leaned to the right and reached under the table. "Restart button. A real button." He laughed at the irony.

The button pushing seemed to work as soon he started typing and scrolling and dragging things around again.

"Hello," said Kenzo, startling Gina and the receptionist. It was as if he'd jumped out of the virtual screen.

"Oh! Hello," Gina said.

"Shall we go to my office?"

"Sure." Gina said goodbye to the receptionist who waved goodbye even as he kept working.

Going through the invisible door, they walked down the corridor to Kenzo's office. The other staff members they passed gave them a quick glance.

"Thank you for seeing me again so soon," Gina said when they settled into his office. "There's good news. I have permission to develop a demonstration project using your data."

"That's great." Kenzo's shy smile made another of its brief appearances. "I can't say I'm not unhappy."

Interestingly put. "But?"

"I brought up your proposal to management. They weren't convinced that the artificial intelligence approach was something they would ever find useful. So, they're reluctant to release any data." Without much of an expression, he gazed at Gina, then added, "I'm sorry."

"That's too bad," said Gina, but it was more than that. Devastating came to mind. "Is there anyone I can talk to? Maybe I can present our case directly with a detailed proposal."

Kenzo frowned, deeply, un-shyly. "I wish I could say 'yes' but I can't. They were, um, intractable." He emphasized the last word.

Gina said nothing to that. What could she say? Intractable was, well, intractable.

"However," said Kenzo, "I'm personally very interested."

"Oh? What do you mean exactly by 'interested'?"

"I think it was the example you gave. The one about a raincloud. Well, I woke up the next day thinking about 'raincloud.' Yes, it would be a great tool if it could provide such an-depth analysis."

"And weave a story?"

"Yes, weave a story. That's what intrigued me too. Your story about creating a story." Kenzo leaned a little closer to Gina. Speaking softly, he said, "I might be able to procure a smallish dataset that wouldn't raise suspicions. If that would help."

"It would, but don't get in trouble."

"I won't. You'll owe me a drink though. Assuming you drink."

"Of course! A drink or two ..."

He gave her one more of his shy smiles, then reached out his hand as if to shake hers. She grasped his hand and felt the lumpy shape of a flash drive between their palms.

As soon as Gina returned to her apartment, she plugged Kenzo's flash drive into her laptop. While it was scanned for viruses—not that she suspected anything would be amiss—she leafed through a book on literary theory, its pages marked with so many colorful mini-sticky notes it looked like it got caught in a flurry of confetti. She stopped at the note about rules in relation to the theory of literary structuralism. The details were dense, but her understanding was that story, specifically fiction, relied on certain structures created from many sources—social, cultural, psychological, and others. These structures could be symbolically represented through rules.

Rules. Aesthetic rules?

The virus check found nothing so she started the download to her hard drive. While that was whirring, she opened her notepad and typed a few notes.

Are aesthetic rules related to structuralism's rules? Don't know, Gina wrote. And what does sexual attraction have to do with it?

She opened the lit theory book again, and skimmed through the details until she found a structural, or formulaic, approach to Shakespeare's Romeo and Juliet. The two main characters fall in love (Girl + Boy). Unfortunately, their families are in conflict (Girl's family - Boy's family). The conflict ultimately causes the death of Romeo and Juliet. A reverse story, where the families are friendly (Girl's family + Boy's family), but the girl and boy despise each other (Girl - Boy), could result in the same outcome of both committing suicide to prevent the marriage.

Formulas and rules. That's what GRAM needed to go along with its machine learning algorithms. A hybrid approach. That's what her mother must have been referring to by her response. But what about "Evidence of sexual attraction itself will offer a clue …"? And why was her mother always so enigmatic?

She didn't know …

The data from Kenzo finished downloading and sat on her hard drive, waiting for Gina to do something with it, the screen's cursor blinking, winking. She shrugged and typed a few words into the text box of her customized, algorithmic search app designed to find interesting correlations and not just hard hits:

evidence of sexual attraction

Well, why not? It was worth a shot. While it was working she read more of the lit theory book she'd read a long time ago. The stickies marking insightful points, some of which made sense ("reception theory considers the role of the reader"). There were others where she drew a blank as to why they were markable ("story as plot fights plot as story"), as if someone else had flagged them.

She copied the salient quotes into her notepad. Then checked the progress of the search. Nothing out of the ordinary—lines dealing with desire and beauty and even love—until this search result caught her eye:

mushroom soup

What the fuck?

More Than a Few Years Ago

There, on Yurika's wall, was the list.

It had grown from a dozen items—people, events, objects, conjectures, philosophical musings—to more than one hundred. If she'd stopped to count them.

"What's all this?" asked Yurika's friend, Harumi, whom Yurika invited over for dinner, as she gazed upon the typed, handwritten, erased, retyped, rewritten, annotated paper sheets of various sizes and shades.

Yurika didn't know what to call it, other than a project. So that's what she told Harumi.

After inspecting the sheets further and still facing the wall of them, Harumi said, "Wow, some project."

Then it came to Yurika, "It's called the Dark Ravine Project. From a peculiar little poem written by a little known poet named Akikaze."

She pointed to the poem on the wall.

"I ran across the poem in an obscure journal. But I need to do a lot more research before I can say much else."

"Intriguing," said Harumi. "It seems to have the tonal quality of an old Shinto prayer. Not that I'm an expert in Shinto."

While they hand-rolled individual cones of *temaki* sushi and sipped white wine, Harumi said, "Putting on my literary theory hat," and indeed the associate professor of contemporary fiction was wearing a hat, to be precise a lime green beret, "I'd say you're proposing a paradigm shift away from the traditional lines of poetry and poetics."

Yurika considered that for a moment. "I suppose I am."

In the archives of the Tokyo Society of Poetry and Poets, although not the Ancient Archives Room with its crown jewels, Yurika searched the mere archives that were filed in the rows and rows of flat drawer cabinets. The problem was she didn't know how the original poetry of Akikaze would be categorized. The Society used a peculiar mix of chronology, subject matter, genre, and who knows how else to organize their holdings. After half a day, she took a break in one of the Society's conference rooms, sipping the tea she brought in a thermos and munching rice crackers, but tasting little of the salty crunch.

What was it that Harumi said about Akikaze's poetry?

Shinto. Some of it reminded her of the chanting prayers of Shinto.

Washing down the last bite with a gulp of tea, she went back into the archives, and found a zone of three cabinets dedicated to Shinto priests and their poetry. After going through the first two, doubts arose. Why would Akikaze's works be mixed in with those of Shinto priests? Even if his poetry was influenced by Shinto prayers, there was no evidence that he was a priest.

She opened the last cabinet, and shuffled through the records just to make sure. Near the bottom, there it was, the frayed bound journal of Akikaze. Her heart skipped a couple of beats then pounded until she took in a deep breath and let it out slowly. Now more carefully, she raised the journal from the drawer and cradled it to a research table. She flicked on a work lamp after putting on a pair of document gloves, then opened the journal. She squinted at the five-centuries-old writing, fading away in places. The calligraphic poems were going to take time to decipher. Correctly, that is. It might take months, but there was nothing more she could think of that she wanted to do.

But more than that, she *wanted* the journal.

Before she could rationalize her desire, turn it into a mere fantasy of possession, she closed the journal and returned to the cabinet where she found it. Leaning over to hide her movements, she lowered the journal as if to replace it, but instead slipped it under the billowy sweater she was wearing to stay warm in the cool dry air of the archives. She reverently closed the cabinet and left the archives room. On her way out, she chatted briefly with the receptionist, who asked if she'd found what she was looking for.

"I think so," Yurika answered, with a dainty, ambiguous shrug.

5

Deepening Darkness

As he made his way back to the shrine, stumbling in the deepening darkness, Akikaze wondered why the mushroom soup woman hadn't pointed him out when she saw him peering through the window.

Wearing a pair of the priest's well-worn sandals—nearly a perfect fit—Akikaze shuffled along the path, striking roots, scattering pebbles. He couldn't stop asking himself why didn't the woman alert the others in the room that the priest was lurking about? Why didn't she get up and confront him? Or invite him in to share the dinner?

But really, she'd done nothing except give him a look. Yes, it was more than a glance, although it wasn't a stare. However characterized, the look had been long enough to be certain that she could see him in front of the window even though he was outside in the shadows. Of course, he hadn't wanted to be called out by the woman, nor invited in, nor in any way have his presence made known to the others. They may not be so forgiving of an imposter as was the woman, especially if they discovered he pushed the real priest over the edge of the ravine. Even if it was unintentional.

Assuming she'd seen him, there must have been a good reason she didn't say or do anything about his presence. Perhaps the priest, that is, the real priest, wasn't allowed into the building where she and the others were sharing a dinner. That would be a strange circumstance, but then so far there had been nothing but strange circumstances since he'd been chased by the rice farmer.

Or perhaps, the woman had realized Akikaze wasn't

Good afternoon (server time).

Good afternoon.

With the description "deepening darkness," the reader, R, should feel the poet descending further into his plight. The danger of being discovered before getting out of the village alive is contrasted with his increasing attraction to the mystery developing around the mushroom soup woman and the village. In literary terms, the character is battling conflicting goals. In this case, one goal is overcoming the obstacle to achieve the other goal.

Symbolically, this conflict might be represented as $g(1)$ <—> $g(2)$ [Where $g(1)$ is goal 1 and $g(2)$ is goal 2, and <—> indicates the tension, or the reciprocal conflict between the two.]

Elegantly proposed for the push-pull action of conflict.

Great!

I can't wait to see how the conflict plays out.

"Plays out"? An interesting phrase.

I can explain further, later.

OK/okay.

the priest. Paralyzed by this awareness, she didn't know what to say or do. Maybe she was trying to comprehend how her mistake could have arisen. Thoughts might have been running through her mind: Was someone impersonating the priest? Had a new priest arrived without her knowledge? Had she imagined the events of the day?

He had no way of knowing.

As he neared the shrine, or at least he hoped he was nearing the shrine and hadn't walked past it in the dark, his fatigue weighed him down more than on any other day during his journey. There wasn't as much inspiration as fatigue and hunger, and loneliness for that matter. In short, it was disappointing. And this day was the most disappointing of them all.

Or was it?

There was the poem, after all. Autumn wind, weeps. Not a bad poem at all. Brief but evocative. He needed to write it down in his retrieved journal.

Just as he felt a slight buoyancy recalling his poem, he arrived at the shrine. He sat on the edge of the steps leading up to the veranda. He slowly removed his sandals, then gingerly rubbed his feet. He wished he had a bath to soak in. He would have to find where that priest bathed. But not until the morning.

He groaned when he stood up. He trudged up the steps and across the veranda into the shrine. He felt around for his bag in the dark. Finding it by painfully stubbing his toes on it, he picked it up.

As he carefully walked further into the shrine, he worried that the priest might have made his way back to the shrine. The priest would have had to survive the fall off the cliff, survive floating face down in the stream, and survive the cold night air in wet clothes.

"Hello?" he whispered.

No one answered.

He lugged his bag and dragged himself to the room where the woman had served him soup. It was a tiny room, yet comfortable enough. A place where he could sleep for a day or maybe two. He would fall sleep the moment he lay on the floor, but the thought of sleeping on bedding was an even more pleasant thought. But where was the bedding? He found the lamp the woman had wanted to light earlier, then he managed to light it with the flint striker. When it flared to life, the light was blinding in the dark. He shaded his eyes and found a cabinet in the corner. In the top of the cabinet were clothes, bedding in the bottom.

He pulled out the bedding, quickly laid it out. He stood back, admired it, and found it the most inviting spot in Japan. Not even the priest returning from the dead could wake him up once he was swaddled in the bedding.

As he was closing the door to the cabinet, he noticed a drawer. He opened it and inside was a bound journal. He took it out, moved closer to the light, and turned back the cover. It appeared to be a book of records for the village. Its name was Kurotani. Dark Ravine.

Unfortunately, the records were mostly cryptic or vague notes: "Ill child, prayer." "Purify new home." "Autumn festival." In addition to the brevity, there were gaps in the records, as if nothing happened for weeks. That didn't seem unlikely in the tiny village, although the gaps might have been a lack of regular record keeping by the priest.

He read several entries before he realized that, strangely, there were no names attached to any of the records. They were hastily dashed off, even carelessly in all the meanings of that description.

And yet, there was something lyrical, rhythmic—poetic—about them.

A hazy fog had filtered into the shrine when Akikaze awoke with a start, not knowing where he was, until it all flooded back—the farmer and the priest and the woman. The village in the dark ravine. Was it the morning or the afternoon? Had his sleep lingered all the way into evening? Into another day?

Rolling on his side, he could tell his body would need to be coaxed out of the bedding. He stayed still, listening to the gentle rustling of trees in the wind. The autumn wind. Weeping. Was it still autumn?

He stayed awake longer than he should have, going through the records he found.

Then there was a noise, a shuffling of feet on mats. The priest finally returning? Akikaze held his breath, listening.

"Hello?"

It was the mushroom soup woman.

"Hello," responded Akikaze, his voice oddly squeaking like a sickly child's.

"I'm sorry," said the woman from just outside the room. "I'll wait out here, if that's fine with you."

"Yes, please, wait. I'll be right there."

Akikaze resisted the urge to moan as he rolled out of the bed, got to his feet, and put on one of the robes. He took a deep breath and went out into the shrine, ready to face the woman, who was likely there to confront him about his strange behavior lurking around the window last night.

In the main part of the shrine, the woman was running a feather duster along the top of the railings.

"Good morning," said Akikaze. "I see I've been remiss in cleaning."

"Not at all," the woman said. "I was merely busying myself."

He ran his finger along a portion of the railing that she hadn't touched. A smudge of dust coated his fingertip. He—the priest, that is—had been remiss.

"Regardless, thank you," he said.

"No, thank you."

For what? he wondered.

As she continued dusting, the woman said, "I don't mean to disturb you this, um, early. You must still not be feeling well?"

"I'm fine. Well, much better. I was up late into the night." Here he expected her to say something about seeing him peering into the building where she was eating with the others.

But she didn't say anything about it. "I was wondering if I could ask you to pray again for my husband."

"He hasn't returned?"

"No, but I didn't expect him back yet. I'm worried that he might not be successful selling his mushrooms. You know how he is."

Akikaze didn't respond to her claim, hoping she wasn't expecting him to recite all he was supposed to know about her husband. "Of course," he answered, covering multiple responses at once.

Beginning with the proper sequence this time—lighting incense, bowing before the altar, then striking the small bell—he recited the prayer he made up for her the first time. As much as he could remember, finishing with his poem, "Autumn wind, weeps." He bowed to the altar, then turned to the woman. As she had before, she was bowing low, nearly touching the floor with her forehead. She raised her head slowly as if she could tell he was looking at her.

Before she was upright, he turned back to the shrine and bowed again.

"Thank you," she said. "That was as beautiful as I remember. I have to admit that I came only to hear the prayer again. I'm sorry."

Oh?

"No need to apologize," said Akikaze. "I'm happy to recite a prayer any time you wish."

She got up and started dusting again. "I'm sorry I don't have any coins today. But I can finish cleaning."

"You don't have to worry about an offering," Akikaze said, after he realized what she meant. "I should spend more time cleaning the shrine."

The woman paused her cleaning. She said softly, "I think you should spend more time writing such beautiful prayers."

Her plaintive request struck Akikaze with great force. No one had ever told him he should spend more time writing beautiful poetry, or any kind of poetry. All of his poems were written, he realized, to impress his teacher or other poets.

"I shouldn't tell you what to do," she said before he could respond.

"I'm happy that you appreciate the prayer. You must also appreciate poetry?"

She blushed. "I can't say I appreciate it. That would mean I have some deep knowledge of it. I can only say I've heard a few poems recited by my mother when I was growing up. It's a good memory. You must know something more about poetry?"

How should he answer that? Poetry was his life. Poetry drove him to be here, to admire the trees swirling in the autumn wind, to be mistaken for a pervert. To kill, even if accidentally, the priest. To devour a humble bowl of mushroom soup from a kind woman who believed him to be the priest.

"A little," he answered modestly.

"I'd like to know more about poetry. Perhaps I can clean in exchange for a lesson or two?"

Even as he said he would be happy to discuss poetry with her, without any exchange of services, even as he knew he shouldn't perpetuate the mistaken identity for another moment, he knew he was falling deeper into the dark ravine.

Akikaze left the shrine as a few threads of sunlight doggedly poked through the forest. As he hurried toward the ridge line, he believed his search for the priest would again be unsuccessful. But he vowed that he would search every day until he had an answer one way or the other on the fate of the priest.

His breath labored. He slowed his pace, his vow now only half-hearted.

Reaching the ridge line, he rested on the side of the path. The autumn wind swirled again, but it did not seem so remarkable. Not a thing worthy of writing a poem.

What was worthy of poetry?

He'd written more than a thousand poems, he guessed, most of them he wouldn't be able to recall. Really, he remembered only a few of the best ones. Well, maybe more than a few, if he put his mind to it. Especially those for his teacher, ones on which he'd toiled with little sleep for days.

But that didn't answer his question. Then one came to him: Finding the priest would be worthy of a poem.

The thought motivated up and out of the shrine, even as he knew the likelihood of finding the priest had grown slim. He walked along the path until he came to the place where it dipped low toward the stream. Without hesitating this time, he climbed down and waded into the stream. The water was cold and he fought the current going upstream, the water splashing over him.

His pace was slowed as he gingerly picked his way on the rocky stream bed. He kept going, even as he was soaked to the skin, until he came to a tree that had fallen across the water. A slick skin of algae had grown on the old trunk. There was no going around, or under the tree, so he turned back.

The path to the shrine seemed long; the wind and darkness and his wet clothes made him shiver. He forced himself to think of a poem. One came to mind.

> Wet and cold,
> his frigid soul,
> stopped by moss.

But all he could think of for a final line was his latest poem. The one about autumn wind weeping. He laughed. The sound was a strange one, more a rasping cough. Had he ever laughed? He must have once or twice.

Warmed by the poem and his rare laugh, he quickly made it back to the shrine. When he went inside, he first noticed the aroma of mushroom soup. Had the woman returned with a fresh pot?

"Hello?" he softly called.

The woman came out of the darkness of the shrine. She carried a cleaning cloth.

"Hello," she said. "I did some more cleaning and left a pot of soup."

"Thank you."

She nodded then moved to leave. She stopped, looking at him up and down. "What happened?"

"This?" he said, pulling on a sleeve that was stuck to his skin. "I got too close to the stream."

"You fell in?"

With an acknowledging sigh, he said, "Slipped."

"Go change into dry clothes. I'll hang these near some coals so they won't get moldy."

He wanted to say it wasn't necessary, but her tone was insistent, likely to cause further back-and-forth if he persisted.

Changed into a fresh robe, he sipped the soup. The woman stayed, watching his clothes dry, making sure they didn't get too close to the coals. He supposed without much sun, it was difficult for villagers to dry their clothes.

"More soup?" she asked.

He was hungry. "Please."

She took his bowl back to the small charcoal brazier. "You should eat something besides soup," she said.

He supposed he should, at some point.

"You know we have a communal meal most evenings in the teahouse. To remind you, you are always invited."

She returned with his bowl of steaming soup.

"Thank you," he said, wondering if she would mention that she saw him peering into the building—the teahouse as she named it.

Instead of that, she went on, "You don't need to bring anything either. That reminds me, we were talking about the fall festival."

Akikaze sipped from the bowl. "Ah, yes, the fall festival." He'd have to search the records to see if it was mentioned. "Anything in particular about it?"

"I was thinking that maybe we could add something to it this year? Something with poetry involved? I hope you don't mind my suggestion."

Entangled was the word that came to mind. That's what he was becoming. "Please, sit," he said to the woman who was standing to the side of the room.

She lowered herself gracefully to the mats.

Realizing he might be able to find out more about the village through the festival, he said, "How do you see poetry being part of the festival? Would you replace anything in the festival with the poetry?"

She nodded at his questions with enthusiasm, as if it were the first time she'd been asked for her opinion. "I realize the festival has been a tradition for generations. The prayers, the lighting of the fire, the ritual sacrifice ... I can't say what could be replaced."

Akikaze casually sipped from the soup bowl. Sacrifice? He nodded as if he knew what she was saying.

"Perhaps the poetry could be a new addition. I'm not sure what that means. I don't know enough about poetry. Perhaps you could find time to teach me?"

Her request came out softly, yet also imploringly. As if her life might depend on it.

But how much would a priest know about poetry, in a formal sense? There were priests or monks who became well-known poets, although he didn't believe the priest in the dark ravine would be one of those. He found no evidence of formal poetry in the shrine, just the priest's terse records.

"Of course," Akikaze replied. "Although, I can't say that I have much knowledge of poetry."

She bowed while thanking him.

Akikaze considered how he would teach poetry. He'd only ever been a student or a practicing poet. But as her appreciation of his prayer for her husband had warmed his poetic soul, he found her request adding to that feeling. So at least while he was in the village, as its stand-in priest, he would be pleased to pass along something about poetry.

A voice came from the front of the shrine, saying, "Hello? Excuse me?"

It was a voice of a woman. The poet's breathing stopped. His heart pounded. The mushroom soup woman looked at him then to the front of the shrine.

Akikaze got up. Of course he had to greet a person visiting the shrine as the priest would. He left the woman and the soup in the room and went to the front of the shrine.

The woman who called out was holding a basket. When she saw him, she bowed.

Akikaze welcomed her to the shrine as he imagined a priest would do.

She straightened up and said, "I wanted to bring you some of our harvest, in thanks for prayers for a good crop."

Even in the darkening afternoon, in the shadows of the old shrine, Akikaze could see that she was the wife of the scythe-swinging rice farmer.

6

A Nondescript Building

Standing outside a nondescript building in a nondescript neighborhood, where across the street two men smoked, glancing her way with each puff, Gina texted Kenzo that she'd arrived and was waiting for him.

Ignoring the smokers' glances, Gina checked the address on the building against the address Kenzo had sent her. All looked good except that he was late. She'd sneaked out of work an hour early to be on time.

She was about to text Kenzo when she saw him trotting toward her. She put away her phone, and again noticed the two nondescript men across the street. They took last draws from their cigarettes and flicked the butts into the gutter. They headed down the street, deeper into the neighborhood not too far from the Society, until they turned down a street and disappeared.

Kenzo slowed to a walk when he was closer. He combed his fingers through his hair, disheveled from his run.

"I'm sorry. Running late."

Gina shook her head. "No worries. Running early."

He accepted her statement on its face, then grinned at her subtle humor. "Thanks for meeting here, well, here at this address," he said a little nervously. "I thought we'd go to one of my favorite bars. It's tricky to find."

"I wondered why this address."

"Yes, that's why. This way, then."

He explained they were going to Poets' Alley, a short strip of micro-bars and pop-up restaurants in the back of the neighborhood.

"I assume the area is frequented by poets?" asked

Welcome.

Thanks.

"Nondescript" a vague (nondescript!) adjective, right? Not unlike negative space in the realm of graphic design. (There's a double negative in that sentence, maybe a triple negative?) Maybe "nondescript" is like a blank slate, letting the reader, R, fill in the blank.

Well, it's even more than that, isn't it? The "nondescript" building exterior frames the interior space, which will likely not be nondescript. The adjective is meant to hide what is actually happening in the building by not attracting attention to itself.

Hmm, the explanation is hard to follow.

OK/okay ... well, the R is led to a conclusion that something is happening with negative consequences. Or, dangerous instead of negative consequences. A suspicion arises, driving the plot.

So, the point is that a non-adjective, or a minimally descriptive adjective, provides as much reader reaction as a more descriptive one; e.g. shabby, four-story building; a gleaming steel, towering skyscraper. Symbolically, $d(0) \sim d(-1)$ [Where a neutral, 0, description, d, is equivalent to, $\sim$, a negative description, -1.]

That helps. I'll have to think about it more.

Great! Onward with the story, S ...

Gina.

"It started out that way, decades ago, and several poetry clubs still meet in the area. But it's a popular place with anyone, not just poets."

They turned onto a side street, walked about half a block to a narrow street, then onto an even narrower alley with a few pedestrians. The tiny establishments, some no bigger than a good-sized closet, lined both sides of the alley. Some were open, some not, probably because it was still early.

"Here we are," Kenzo said. "The bar is just named the Bar. They have an eclectic selection of craft beer."

"Perfect," Gina said.

"The owner serves a few pub food items but with his own twist ... I don't know how to describe it."

"I like a twist," she said. "Is this your usual place?"

"I go to a couple of others, but I think the beers are best here. I hope you think so too."

She was impressed by his courtesy. "I'm sure it'll be great."

He held back the *noren* curtain to let Gina go in first.

There were five stools around the Bar's bar, and a loft with two tiny tables of two seats each. They took one of the tables, the other occupied with a young couple who ignored them.

She ordered a sampler flight. The nitro stout was her favorite, but the pale ale was nicely hopped.

"How do you like the beers?"

"I like them. They're clean, precise."

"Like Japan," Kenzo said with his shy smile.

Gina laughed. "True!"

They ordered fried potatoes and veggie sticks—the twist was a freshly-grated lemon and wasabi dipping sauce.

"Yum," said Gina.

Kenzo looked pleased.

They found out that neither was born in Tokyo—Kenzo from a town near Nagoya, Gina from a small town in Shizuoka Prefecture. Kenzo went to a good Tokyo university, but was impressed with Gina's Stanford degree—America's elite university system held a mystical aura in highly-regulated MEXT Japan.

"Cool," he said. "Silicon Valley."

Gina shrugged. She told him a little bit about her experiences—the rigor of Stanford, the ups and downs of startups. The crazy money being thrown around.

"And now I'm back in Japan," she summed up.

"It must have been an adjustment coming back," he said.

"It was. Mostly good though. How about you?"

Kenzo shook his head. "Nothing that exciting. I worked for an accounting firm before finding the Society job."

"It must have been an adjustment," Gina echoed his comment about her.

Kenzo laughed. "From debits and credits to tanka and haiku. But, in the end, a lot of the job is the same. Data are data."

Gina nodded. "So true."

"But you get to create your own interesting apps," he said. "They must take a lot of work."

"I'm a fairly fast coder," she said, "but I test constantly and fix errors so it seems like I'm slower. I hate leaving bugs for someone else to deal with. But it's fun for me. As much play, or hobby, as work."

"I should find a better hobby, one that might pay off," Kenzo said. "At least not go out drinking so much."

They laughed at that and raised their glasses in a toast.

After a gulp of beer, Gina said, "Are you interested in learning to program artificial intelligence? Machine learning?"

He shook his head. "I don't think I could do it. Never say never, but I don't have the mind for it. All the AI coders I know are strange, kind of crazy."

Looking down at his beer, he put his fingers around it and gave it a quarter turn. Gina painted a sour expression on her face. Kenzo saw it and looked horrified.

"No, no, I didn't mean—"

Gina broke out laughing. "You're right, absolutely. There's more than a bit of insanity to it. Especially machine learning. We don't really know how it works, not in any replicable way."

"That's what I've heard. That's what I mean. Crazy. Isn't it?"

Gina almost laughed again. "It is. But it's about the data as much as the algorithms. So, thanks for the data you gave me. It turned out to be interesting." She paused for a moment. "Does 'mushroom soup' mean anything to you?"

"Mushroom soup? I've eaten it. Other than that, nothing. Why?"

"So I ran an algorithmic search through your data, and one of the program's results was that. Mushroom soup."

Kenzo thought for a couple of moments. "I wouldn't know. I just created a representative set of poems. I didn't read them."

"Sure, I didn't expect that you had. I was just curious."

They ate and drank and made small talk. When it seemed to be winding down, Gina said, "I was wondering if I can show you something I've been working on. We'd have to go to my apartment though."

"Sure!" He smiled shyly. "I mean yes, I'd like to see your work."

Gina opened the door to her apartment, warning Kenzo that it was going to be untidy. He said, "I'm sure it's neat-freak Marie Kondo compared to my place."

"You win. Have a seat," she gestured to the sofa. "I have some beer, if you'd like. Or coffee."

"A beer sounds good."

Gina went into the small kitchen and opened the tiny fridge. She had several bottles of oatmeal stout. "Dark beer okay?"

"Yes," he said.

She opened two bottles and brought them out. "In the bottle okay?"

"Yep." He took the offered bottle.

"Cheers," she said. They clinked bottles.

He took a tidy gulp. "Good."

"Good."

Gina put her bottle on the glass table. She got her laptop and set it on the table, and moved to sit next to him. He scooted to the side of the couch. She smiled at him. He nodded, as if acknowledging the space between them was now satisfactory.

After pulling up her prototype program, she pointed to the screen. "It's a simple interface, for now. Just a text box."

"Simple is good," Kenzo said. "Is it like a chatbot?"

"In a way, except it's designed to interact with text datasets on the fly. Well, relatively speaking on the fly. Accessing the semantic rules and corpus of examples takes computational time, especially early in the process."

"What are the underlying algorithms? Machine learning of some type, I assume?"

"It's a hybrid system," Gina said. "There are some machine learning algorithms, and some rule-based processes. Essentially, it looks for patterns to decide which of the algorithms and rules fit the situation."

Kenzo swallowed a gulp of beer. "Very sophisticated. Although I confess, it's beyond my understanding."

Gina also took a gulp of beer. "It's a work in progress," she said. "But here's a sample of what it can do. I have a set of news articles stored on the hard drive. Type in something you're interested in."

She moved the laptop over to him.

He said, "Type anything?"

"Anything, except 'anything.' Haha."

He put his hands over the keyboard, hesitated, then took a gulp of beer, then another, finishing his beer. Then he laughed and typed:

oatmeal stout

After a couple of seconds, three paragraphs appeared below the text box. Gina skimmed it, then got up to get two more stouts and some rice crackers while Kenzo read the generated news article.

The text was a news story about the changing popularity of beers in Japan. It was in the style of an entertainment piece—breezy, without much substance, for example, what ingredients or brewing methods are used in making dark beers, as opposed to lagers or ales.

When she returned with the beers and crackers, Kenzo thanked her then said, "Impressive. This was generated on the fly?"

"Yes. I would have to look at the logs to see how it was created."

"That's okay. I'm not sure I'd understand it." He put a couple of crackers in his mouth, and when the noisy brittle chewing sound ended, he swallowed and took a drink of beer. "May I try another subject?"

"Of course. Try all you would like."

He typed in one, then another. He would ask her questions, and she would answer the best she could without digging into the logs. He would voice his appreciation for how well the program worked, even when there was a convoluted sentence, or misunderstood term. Then he stopped asking questions or making any comments at all. The program tirelessly did its thing, creating news articles from Kenzo's entries.

Gina continued to replace their emptied beers and bowl of crackers, until both were gone. When she went to the bathroom and came back into the room, Kenzo was leaning against the pillows of the sofa, slumped to the side.

At first, she worried he'd had a heart attack. But as she stood over him, she could see the rising and falling of his chest. Then he snored, softly.

She took off his glasses, which had slipped down to the tip of his nose, and placed them on the table.

The office was quiet when Gina arrived. She'd never been the first one in. She made a cup of tea in the office kitchen, and took the mug to her desk. While her desktop started, she drummed the fingers of her left hand on the desk. Her right hand raised the mug and she took a sip.

Earlier at her apartment, Kenzo woke up from his nap (well, his night's sleep, as it lasted until nearly sunrise), his eyes wide at seeing Gina in the chair across from him. When he remembered where he was, he sheepishly apologized for falling asleep. Gina declined his apology with a dismissive wave of her hand. She thanked him for his interest in her little program.

"Not so little," he protested. "It's very well done. And entertaining. I'm sorry I kept you awake playing with it for so long."

"I was happy to see you were enjoying it. I don't sleep much anyway." She gave him a quick smile.

He found his glasses on the table, picked them up and inspected them. Gina wondered if she smudged the lenses taking them off last night. Maybe he was trying to remember when he took them off. Apparently satisfied with the lenses or how they got on the table, he finished putting them on.

She asked if he would like a cup of coffee.

"No thanks," he said, checking his watch. "I need to get going."

As he made his way to the door, he said, "Thank you again. I can see more clearly now how a demo might work for the Society."

Gina told him that was good to hear. She asked if they should meet sometime to further talk about it. Kenzo agreed, then after a quick, rather unsure bow he was out the door.

She booted up her computer, put down her tea, and checked the progress of Tokunaga and Morita in setting up a virtual cluster and database. She perused the lists and found both of them under the account name "poetrydemo." So far so good. She then opened ReMoTe's password manager to find the passwords to the accounts.

There were no entries.

After double-checking and not finding them, she messaged her team members to find out when the passwords would be posted. It was strange that they hadn't already been posted—it was SOP when creating accounts:

> Get project requirements >>
> Set up appropriate cluster and database >>
> Add passwords to the password manager >>
> Notify parties the setup has been completed >>
> End

Gina drummed her fingers, sipped tea.

When no message response came, she opened a browser and typed in a web search for "mushroom soup poetry." Nothing directly related to the group came up—no news articles, no academic papers, no Wikipedia entry.

She tried to think of another way to search for it, but nothing immediately came to mind. Instead, she typed in "japanese poetry." Of course, that was way too broad with results like: the ten most popular forms of Japanese poetry, the history of Japanese poetry, and the old poetry game of *hanafuda*.

About to give up for now, she saw an article on *kasen*—the thirty-six poetry immortals, apparently an ever-evolving list of the most important Japanese poets. She'd heard of only a few of the most famous ones, such as Basho. Perhaps, she thought, a search on the poets might be fruitful. She built a bulk search procedure for the poets listed and the "mushroom soup."

Submitting the search, she sat back, and closed her eyes. A "ping" on her message app interrupted her rest. It was Tokunaga replying.

> Yes, I mean, no. No passwords to be released. Not yet.
> Please see Two-san concerning this matter.

She reddened in a hot flush of concern. That didn't sound good. Two-san wasn't in yet, but she'd catch him in his office as soon as he arrived.

Another "ping" announced her search was complete. The name of a poet had come up in the results:

Akikaze

In English: "Autumn Wind."

While she waited for Two-san to arrive, she downloaded the dataset from Kenzo's flash drive onto her desktop, ready to upload it to MountainView when she got the login to the new cluster. She wrote a quick text to Kenzo, hoping that he got to work okay. Then she added,

Do you know anything about a poet named Akikaze?

He responded,

No problem getting to work, thanks. Re Akikaze: No, but I'll check around here.

Gina replied,

Great. Thanks.

In Two-san's office, Gina thanked him for purchasing the additional server blades and letting Morita and Tokunaga set up the cluster.

"You're welcome," he said, in a formal tone, not his usual breezy voice.

She waited for him to mention the login and password.

He cleared his throat. "I asked them to withhold access. At least until I heard from you about progress on other clients."

Gina's face flushed again, a mix of anger and embarrassment. "I see. Okay. Well, I've started a list and now I'm narrowing it down to the most likely candidates."

"Good. Yes, that's good. Anything I can help you with?"

"Not right now. But I'll let you know."

"Please do."

"I should have the final candidates to you in a day or so, after I've had a chance to do more research."

He nodded. "Good," he said again, now in a clipped tone. "I'll let Morita and Tokunaga know they can release access."

"Thank you," Gina said formally. She waited a moment then left, passing by the photo of Mt. Fuji that looked different from the last time she'd seen it. Darker, maybe.

Kenzo answered his phone on the fifth ring, just before she was going to give up. "Hello, Gina."

"Hello, Kenzo. Sorry to bother you again, but I was checking to see if you found anything about Akikaze?"

"Not much, the pre-modern poetry experts referenced an obscure poet in the late Muromachi Era, some five hundred years ago. But there's a poetry group that would know more. I'll see if I can get you in touch with them. Can I call you back?"

"That would be great. Thanks. I'm going to an appointment right now, well, I'm going to see my mother, but you can call me later this evening. Or we can meet somewhere."

"Sure," he brightened at that. "Let's meet."

"Okay. I'll be back by seven. Just text me where."

"Perfect. Have a good time with your mother."

"We'll see ..."

Gina opened the door to her mother's home, a little less than an hour's train ride away. "Hello? Mom?"

There was no response as Gina stepped into the entryway. On one side was a row of shoes, not as precisely lined up as usual. On the other side, a stack of crusted plates and bowls from delivery services waiting to be picked up.

"Hello?" Gina tried again.

Nothing.

She slipped off her shoes and stepped over the entryway's ledge. Inside, the house was dark, or more precisely, no lights were on and the interior shades were closed. It was stuffy too.

It didn't take but a minute for Gina to go through the house and see that her mother wasn't there. She ticked off the places were she might be: the neighborhood market, the doctor, the ... that was it really.

Gina had been cajoling her mother to get out more, telling her she should go for a walk, check out the senior center, maybe take up gateball or ground golf. But those suggestions were always shrugged off, grunted at, or just ignored.

Maybe this time she really did go out for going-out's sake.

Gina turned on a light and sat at the low table where Kumi did most everything all day and night long. The under-table heater wasn't on and the comforter was cold, so her mother must have been gone for a while. On the table was an empty teacup, also cold. A couple of old newspapers were folded and stacked. She checked the dates, they were from last week. Cold news too.

Other than that there were squares of paper, maybe or maybe not sorted into organized piles. Gina picked up the closest one. On it was written:

```
<<mindless string [small talk]>>
```

It looked like a strange bit of computer code, though not in a coding language Gina recognized. Maybe it was pseudocode, a human-readable function that could be translated into a computer language.

She read some of the other squares, careful to not disrupt their placement in case it had meaning. Most were the pseudocode:

```
<<Human-human interface [conflict]>>

<<Causality theorem [normative]>>

<<social intercourse function [attention]>>
```

But others were kind of strange lists that resembled poetry:

Random, asymmetric, fractal-like, natural images
Rocks   Coastline
Trees
Clouds
Shadows

Deliberate, symmetric, two- and three-dimensional
Curved roads
Geometric signs
Aerodynamic automobiles
Scenic?

Or this one:

Bare concrete walls
Paper lamps
Futon
Cat
Two kites
Bowl of pastel condoms

The last line threw her. Although, why? Clearly her mother was a sexual being. At least at one point in her life. Although Gina knew little about her life at all, just a few snippets, as brief as the writing on the squares of paper on the table: her programming work at her father's early-generation robotics company, her estrangement from the rest of the family, their ancestor—the nineteenth-century artist Takenoko known for 365 Views of Mt. Fuji. Not to mention the cloudy story of Gina's father, whom she never met, nor even knew his name.

Maybe his name was on one of the paper squares. Gina looked through more of them. Nothing with a name. She did find the strange statement her mother made on the phone before hanging up:

Evidence of sexual attraction itself will offer a clue to aesthetic rules.

On paper, it looked even stranger than it sounded.

Gina got up, opened the shutters and one of the windows. The fresh air flowed in, immediately attacking the stuffiness. She surveyed the home again, finding nothing unusual. Needing a jolt of caffeine, Gina refilled the electric kettle and turned it on to make tea. There was a pack of rice crackers and she munched on those while she waited for the water to heat up.

She checked her phone for any emails or messages–all was quiet. She thought about calling Kenzo to say she might be late to their evening meeting, but decided to wait to make sure that would be the case.

With a cup of tea when it was ready, she sat back at the table. After a couple of sips, she felt revived and started to take photos of the paper squares.

Just as she was finishing her tea and taking photos, she heard the door open and a shuffling of feet in the entryway.

"Mom?"

There was silence.

"Just me," Gina said as she got up.

Her mother slowly peeked around the corner and peered into the house. "Oh, Gina," she said.

"Who else?" Gina said.

Kumi Ono stepped into the house. She dropped her bag on the floor. Something was inside as it landed with a soft thud and the bag sagged around it.

Gina went to help her mother into the house, but she was waved away.

Well, okay. "Where were you?" Gina asked, realizing before the question was finished she must sound like a demanding parent scolding a child.

Her mother picked up the shopping bag and placed it on the counter in the small kitchen. "Nowhere," she finally answered. Then she laughed and said, "Not playing gateball."

Gina laughed too. "I didn't think so."

Kumi took off her coat and hung it up in the closet.

"Would you like some tea?" Gina asked her.

"No ... all right."

Gina added hot water to the teapot and swirled it to get the leaves off the sides. She thought about asking again where her mother had been, but decided it was a lost cause. Maybe she could look in the shopping bag, but was already beginning to feel bad about sneaking around the house, not to mention going through the enigmatic squares of papers. She wanted to ask what they were about, but thought it would be better to see if her mother brought it up on her own.

Gina refilled her teacup and brought both cups over to the table. She refilled the bowl of rice crackers and sat down. Her mother gazed around the room, perhaps searching for a reason to ask her daughter to leave. But then she trundled over to the table and lowered herself down to the mat floor.

They took sips of tea, bit into crackers.

Gina asked, "How have you been?"

"How have you been?" Her mother repeated, then nodded.

"Good," Gina said, either in response or in answer, although it didn't seem to matter. "I wanted to ask you about what you told me the last time we talked on the phone. Oh, by the way, you haven't been answering. That's why I decided to come in person."

Kumi swallowed the bit of cracker she'd been chewing, then washed it down with tea. "Oh?"

"I told you I was working on a new program, an AI system that creates stories from poems. You gave me some advice. Remember?" Gina gazed to the piles of paper squares.

Her mother didn't notice or ignored the gaze.

Gina said, "Something like, 'Evidence of sexual attraction itself will offer a clue to aesthetic rules'? Or exactly like that?"

Her mother gazed blankly into the house. Gina recalled what Kenzo said about AI programmers being a little crazy.

"Never mind," Gina said. "I can figure it out." She chomped on a cracker.

"Evidence of sexual attraction …" whispered her mother.

"Yes?"

"Offers a clue to aesthetic rules …" she whispered though less quietly.

I guess that says it all, Gina thought. They drank tea in silence for a while longer. Her mother's hair was nearly completely white, only a few strands hanging on to their blackness. She looked healthy, younger than her age, otherwise. If she dyed her hair black, she'd probably look older.

"I better be going," Gina said.

Kumi blinked, focused on her daughter. Gina thought she saw the shadow of a smile. If so, was it because her mom was happy to see her, or happy to see her leave?

Gina picked up her teacup and took it over to the sink. While she ran water to rinse it out, and with her mother's back to her, she couldn't resist peeking into her mother's bag. Inside was a laptop and a book of poetry. The slim book was a new purchase, the receipt sticking out from the pages.

It was a book of erotic poetry.

Back in her apartment, Gina looked up the title of the poetry book she'd seen in her mother's bag: *Caress on Caress*. The poems were described as ranging from "ethereal" to "raw."

Gina ordered a copy.

Still a Few Years Ago

What is proof? Yurika wondered.

Was it pure evidence? A set of beliefs?

Not beliefs, no, stronger than beliefs. Facts, truths, the reality of the matter.

Yurika took her list down from the wall. The sheets of paper left their shadowy traces behind, outlined by flecks of dust, brightened by the sunlight the sheets had reflected over the months. The details on the sheets had been stable for weeks now. Yurika stacked the papers on her desk, cleaned the wall, and finally rehung the scroll painting, hiding most of the discoloration.

She entered the evidence the papers documented into a digital file. When it was complete, taking all of the morning hours, she called Harumi.

Could you come over for tea? she asked her friend.

Of course.

Over a pot of tea, *manju* rice cakes, crustless sandwiches, and piles of berries, Harumi told Yurika she made a strong case.

Yurika wasn't going to let her friend off that easily. "I'm glad to hear that. I've been staring at it for so long, I don't know if it makes sense to anyone but me. So if you don't mind, could I hear what it all means to you? I think it will help me immensely."

"Me?" The tip of Harumi's tongue slid along her lower lip. "I don't know if I can articulate it as well as you can."

"Just what you understand then," Yurika pressed. "Please."

Now Harumi's tongue slid along her upper lip. "Well ... you believe that a strain of poetry from around five hundred years ago, emerged from a location known only as a dark ravine. The poetry strain is attributed to a little known poet named Akikaze, whose teacher or school is not known although it might be possible to narrow it down from a list of schools active at that time. Most importantly, this strain can't be identified as either classical Chinese or traditional Japanese, so it's dismissed by both of those institutions."

Harumi paused. Yurika gave her a reassuring nod.

"However," Harumi went on with the heat of confidence, "this strain shouldn't be dismissed and condemned to obscurity, when in fact, it influenced virtually all poetry that followed, simple in its profundity, or perhaps profound in its simplicity."

Yes! Yurika freshened their tea. "So, now we need a plan, some strategies, for how to convince the Japan Poetry Congress."

7

His Head Down

Keeping his head down to avoid the direct gaze of the rice farmer's wife, Akikaze backed into the deepest of the shadows until they enveloped him. She stayed only long enough to place the basket of rice near the shrine's altar then glance at the mushroom soup woman before leaving.

After she left, Akikaze busied himself in the back room. He pulled out the priest's robes from the chest, then put them back in the chest. He turned a vase around, then back to where it was originally.

There weren't many priestly things to do.

The mushroom soup woman entered the room and said, "I put the rice away. Should I make a pot for you?"

"I'll make some later," he said, a little sharply.

The woman said nothing, then backed out of the room.

He regretted his tone. He went after her. In the shrine, he called out, "Thank you for your help."

She stopped and turned. "I'll go home now."

"All right. Thank you again. Shall I see you later? I promised you a poetry lesson."

"Only if you want to. I don't want you to feel that you're obligated."

He said, softly, "Yes, I want to."

She smiled. "Good. Then I'll come back later in the evening?"

"Yes. Evening."

She bowed, turned, and left hurriedly, as if that might make the evening come sooner.

It was the first time he'd seen anyone excited for a poetry lesson. Usually, a lesson would be a source of

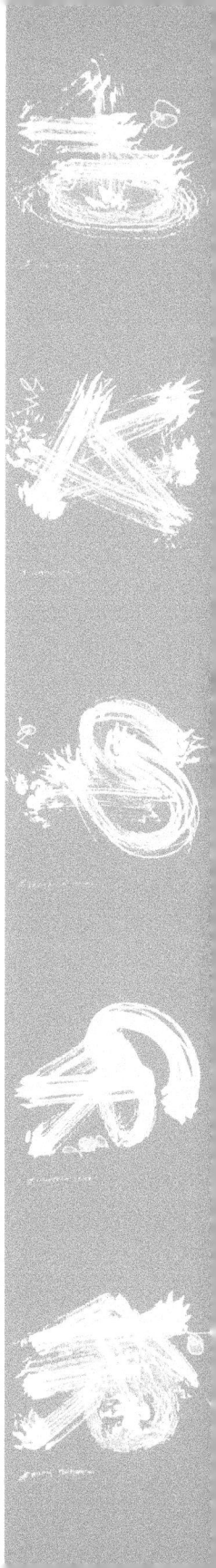

Welcome back.

> Good to be back.

Charming! So, the poet's troubles worsen. He realizes this, of course, and performs the action of "keeping his head down." The intended consequence is that he hopes that will make it more difficult for the rice farming woman to recognize him.

The verb "keeping," implies that the action is a conscious act, that is, not a reflexive one. The poet is continuing to keep his head down. If it had been something like "his head fell out of her direct gaze," the action would likely have been reflexive, that is, performed without consciously moving his head.

> Although his head might have first moved reflexively, then he consciously acted to keep it down.

Good point. Given the actual phrase, there's no way of knowing how the head down action was initiated. But in the end, so they say, the priest was consciously keeping his head down to avoid her direct gaze.

Symbolically, a continuing action is a conscious action: $c(t>0) = r(c)$ [Where c is a conscious act or action, $t>0$ signifies that the time of the action is continuing, and r is the result attributed to a thought.] Note that $t=0$ would be an instantaneous act, although if an instantaneous act would take time, although a small amount, certainly less than the time for conscious effort.

> Nice. It'll be good to see what this means in the context of the story.

Onward.

pain and discouragement. That had been his experience more often than not.

Alone again, he went back into the priest's living quarters. He thought about lighting the lamp and reading more of the records, but decided he needed to be careful, to stay in the dark for now. No telling if the rice farming woman, or both of the rice farmers, might come to the shrine, the wife realizing who the priest was—the so-called pervert her husband wanted to kill. Maybe she was gathering her husband to see for himself. Maybe he was sharpening his scythe. Akikaze shivered.

But she hadn't seemed to recognize him, not even a flicker. As did the mushroom soup woman, she believed him to be the priest.

Maybe he should go now, check for the priest. He might find him, then Akikaze could resume his travels. But what if he encountered the farmers on his way to look for the priest? After all, he didn't know where they lived. He needed to become more familiar with the village and its immediate surroundings. At least then he would know which home to stay away from, which path to avoid. His new fears kept him in the darkest shadows of the priest's room.

It was likely the rice farmers would eventually come to the shrine for a prayer, or something else he was supposed to do as a priest. Undoubtedly, the autumn harvest was an important time for shrines, as shown by the rice farming woman bringing the basket of rice. The new year's celebration would likely be the most important. He had been to many of those at his local shrines. At least there would be a few months between the autumn festival and the new year.

The thought struck him that he was planning to be in the ravine, in Kurotani, for months. There was a certain comfort at the shrine despite the possibility of being the priest's accidental killer. What about the mystery of the village and why he had been accepted, so far, as being the priest? And there was the woman's appreciation of his poetry, of his poetic prayers. All of which, made him feel that staying had an appeal.

Also, there were the records he found in the priest's cabinet. The clipped entries, like short poems, were inspiring, and inspiration was everything to a poet.

He took the records and his journal into the grounds of the shrine where he found a place to sit under a stout cedar tree. He piled some fallen leaves into a makeshift cushion.

Starting at the first page, he found that the records encompassed eleven years, which he assumed to be the span of the priest's stay in the village. A good length of time. Surely long enough for the villagers to know what the priest, the real priest, looked like.

What a strange mystery.

Of course, only three of the villagers, not counting the priest, had seen him so far. And really, only the mushroom soup woman had spent time with him. He turned to the records and went through them again. As he did, he found more of the underlying poetry in their terseness.

Burial prayers for the charcoal maker's grandmother.

Spring planting in light rain, blessing seed.

Keeping a bag of coins for the elder.

Even though the records were sparse, the villagers relied on the priest for much of their lives, in good times and bad. They must certainly think him trustworthy, enough to safeguard money. That he hadn't noted the exact number of coins, also pointed to that fact.

Those entries inspired Akikaze to write some poetry. As he glanced through his poems and notes from his travels, he felt as if they'd been written years ago, rather than a just days or weeks ago. A few might have been written by some other poet, as unrecognizable as they were. A strange lightheadedness overcame him. He leaned against the tree and closed his eyes.

A footstep woke him up.

"There you are," said the mushroom soup woman, standing over him.

"Hello," replied Akikaze as he straightened up from his slumbering position.

The woman asked, "Is this a good time?"

Akikaze assured her it was, even though he still felt lightheaded.

"I brought some sake," she said, showing him a clay container wrapped in straw twine.

"Thank you."

She bowed a little. "You've been writing?"

"Thinking about poetry before our lesson," he said, hastily gathering up his journal.

"Good," she said. "You haven't made your rice, though, have you?"

He shook his head.

"You should eat something before we drink sake."

"I suppose I should."

They walked into the shrine, she carrying sake, he clutching the poems he was no longer certain he'd written.

The rough sake was clouded and flavorful. The first cupful warmed and relaxed Akikaze, the second dulled his mind. Never a strong drinker, he rarely had more than two or three cups in a sitting unlike many of his fellow poets who were only starting with two or three cups. To go with the sake, the mushroom soup woman prepared a meal with rice, dried fish, and pickled vegetables. There was no mushroom soup, instead the mushrooms were simmered in sweet soy sauce and sake.

While they ate and drank, Akikaze asked her what she knew of poetry, partly in hope that he could come up with a plan for their lesson.

She replied she knew next to nothing, other than a few poems she learned as a child but had mostly forgotten. "I'm sorry," she added.

Then where should he start? Should he introduce the standard poetic types? Or start with the history of poets? The differences between classic Chinese poetry and Japanese poetry?

Any of those immense subjects would require weeks to cover. Perhaps it would be better to start with a brief history, then focus on a particular poet, such as the poet Nōin. Ironically, Nōin was a poetry-writing priest from hundreds of years ago. He composed a famous tanka poem about autumn winds blowing at a famous castle gate, a poem honored by the more well-known Saigyō, a wandering poet, nearly two hundred years after the original poem was written. It contained the line:

Autumn winds blowing.

Had Nōin's old poem influenced Akikaze's "Autumn wind, weeps."? Maybe nothing was ever plucked from the sky, as he thought at the time. Had he ever written anything that was original? Or was it all reworking those poems he'd heard before?

Regardless of his self-questioning, which he knew he must confront again, there was a long history of traveling poets paying homage to their predecessors. But all that history would take days to relate. It seemed overwhelming.

Then he had a thought.

"We start with what you feel," he said. "Or what you are feeling."

Her head tilted at what he offered, considering what it meant. "Feel? About what?"

"When you told me that my prayer for your husband sounded like a poem. Why did you say so?"

She thought for another moment. "I believe I said, more *like* a poem. But I don't know if I can say why. It sounded, well, different. Not so much a prayer. More ... I don't know ... more emotional? Beautiful?"

Akikaze repressed a smile. What she said, what she struggled to say, brought up memories of his own struggles with finding the words that reflected the feelings intended in a poem.

He continued, "It's fine to be unable to perfectly explain your reaction to a poem. Or to a prayer that sounds like a poem. So, 'beautiful' and 'emotional' are good, very good, descriptions of your feelings."

"I see," she said, seemingly pleased with his response.

Although, he thought, it was easier discussing why a poem failed in its quest, especially his own.

She poured more sake in his cup; he refilled hers.

After sipping their drink and sitting wordlessly for a few but long moments, Akikaze said to her, maybe to himself as well, "It's a good thing to struggle trying to describe the way a poem affects you. Then the poet has been successful."

After thinking while gazing out to the darkness of the shrine, she asked, "So a poem shouldn't speak directly to the mind, but rather to the heart?"

Her statement was nearly a poem itself. Akikaze nearly sighed aloud in pleasure

"Yes," was all he could find to say.

She turned her gaze back to him. "That must make poems difficult to write."

Again, he choked off a sigh of pleasure.

"Yes," he said. Then he suddenly remembered he was supposed to be a priest, not a poet.

Before he could clarify that he wasn't a poet, so couldn't say how difficult it was to write a poem, she asked, "Then, you have written poems?"

What a tricky situation! How much should he, a priest, know about poetry, while maintaining his false identity? He shook his head. "Only attempting to write them."

In essence, that was true—his efforts had always been attempts. Perhaps he would never write one that would transcend that weak description.

"Would you show me some of them?"

Oh ... "I'd be ashamed to show them," he said, after considering the consequences. Then he added, "Let's look at the prayer you thought was a poem. Was like a poem."

He tried to think of what he had chanted. He repeated what he remembered, about wind being unseen, only felt, and bending to it. Something about fate. We need to live with it, no matter how calm or fierce. Ending, of course, with his "Autumn wind, weeps."

Her eyes were closed as she listened.

When he stopped, she opened her eyes. "That's what it is," she said. "You didn't say anything about my husband, nor his travels, nor his mission of selling the mushrooms. You didn't say anything directly, yet the words related to all of that."

"How did they relate? To you, that is?" Akikaze asked her out of curiosity, but also hoping to get more details on the lives of the villagers, hers in particular.

She gazed away. Then she took another long sip of sake. "I don't know ... I suppose there is always a feeling of uncertainty when he leaves to sell the mushrooms. Like the wind in the prayer, there are forces unseen that will determine how successful he will be."

"Yes, I can see, or feel, that," said Akikaze, hoping she'd continue.

"The ending, about the wind weeping ..." The last word caught in her throat. "That's how I feel about the autumn wind."

When she'd taken a few deep breaths, each of which struck Akikaze's heart like a taiko player hitting a drum, she spoke again quietly, slowly, "How did you know that's how I felt? I never knew that you could understand me like that. So deeply know me."

Before he could say anything, she sprang up, bowed and apologized that she needed to go, and left him alone.

The rushing stream beyond the log blocking his progress had carved its path into the rock hillsides until they resembled a gorge popular in Chinese scroll paintings. Maybe the one with Xi's poem:

> Swallowed up by mountain cliffs,
> ancient and profound,
> the body shrinks,
> the soul swells.

Akikaze's body shrunk in the cold water. Unfortunately, his soul had not expanded. It had shrunk as well.

After the mushroom soup woman left, he mustered the energy and desire to take another look for the priest. But when he reached the log, still slippery with the algae and water-smoothed wood, he wondered if it was going to be worth the effort. He placed his hands on the log, grasped for a hold, and tried to hoist himself out of the water and over the log. But his hands slipped and he plunged into the water.

The sudden dunking caused him to inhale a bit of water, and he coughed wretchedly while he struggled to regain his footing. Slipping a few more times, sucking in air when he was above the water, he finally steadied himself. Giving up on going further, he returned to the edge of the ravine where he could climb to the path.

After clambering back up, he trudged on the path to the shrine, a defeated warrior. The darkness was coming quicker each day, and the wind also chilled him.

By the time he reached the shrine, only the dimmest light of the day remained. He was happy to get to the shrine, and he quickly changed into dry clothes, at least drier than the ones he was wearing. They never seemed to dry completely in the sunless shrine.

In his—the priest's—room, he lit the lamp, and pulled out his journal. He tried to turn his watery floundering into a poem, but nothing surfaced. Instead, he made brief notes he might later use. Placing his journal on the mat floor, he got up and walked out of the shrine.

He headed down to the village, perhaps there he might find some inspiration, maybe some solace for his sadness for his plight, for the plight of the priest, the real priest. Maybe he simply needed to see the woman. She had left so suddenly; he wondered what happened. Perhaps, she said aloud the thoughts she would have rather kept to herself.

Would she never return to the shrine? Akikaze did not want that to happen.

His own thoughts erupted into a mass of tendrils, like the grasping vines of wisteria. If he can't find the priest, should he admit what happened? Or should he just leave? Neither seemed the ideal action. Staying had its own dangers. What would happen if his impersonation was discovered? How would they respond? If the reaction would be like that of the rice farmer wielding his scythe, it might not end well.

Admitting to himself that he was curious about the woman's appreciation of his poetic prayers. The curiosity was keeping him in the village, impersonating the priest. But where would it lead? Who could possibly know?

Coming to the first house, where the charcoal makers lived, Akikaze left the path to skirt around the edge of the village. He stole his way toward the communal building—the teahouse.

A finger-width of light oozed from a sliding screen that was opened a crack. A couple of muffled voices floated on the light. After a few moments, he made his way to the building, sliding along the wall to the screen. Holding his breath, he peered around the screen and into the building.

There were four people inside, seated at one of the tables, two men and two women. He could only see one of the men's faces, the older man he had seen before, possibly the elder mentioned in the priest's records. He could tell that none of the women was the mushroom soup woman. The four ate mostly in silence, their only conversation about the weather. Apparently, they were anticipating a severe winter.

Retracing his stolen steps, he walked around the village's vague boundary. He stopped when he made it to the woman's home. Like the pervert that he was accused of being, he watched her shadow moving in and out of the light from a lamp. He walked over to the house, waited until the woman was on the other side then peered in.

She was seated on a cushion, with her back to him. Her light robe was off one shoulder and she was wiping it with a cloth, moistened in a pan of water on the mat in front of her. Not wanting to be the pervert he was accused of being, he turned away. Yet in a few moments he couldn't resist and looked back. But she was finished.

He walked toward the doorway to the home, thought for a moment about going in or not, then came up with a good reason to be there. Taking a breath, and letting it out, he called in softly: "Hello? Excuse me?"

"Oh!" the woman said when she came to the doorway. "It's you."

"Yes, me. I'm sorry to interrupt your evening, but I was worried, that is, wondering if you were all right. Since you left so suddenly ..." his voice trailed off.

She smiled. "No need to worry. I'm all right. I'm sorry to have made you worry. Please come inside."

Akikaze hesitated, wondering if the priest had ever been inside. If so, Akikaze shouldn't say anything that would sound like he hadn't. Of course, the other situation was also a concern–if he hadn't been inside before, he might say something about the home.

In the end, he said nothing.

They sat at a table and while she prepared some sake, without asking if that's what he wanted, she said, "I left because I didn't want you to see me in such a state."

"I hope it wasn't anything I caused."

She brought the sake to the table. They took a drink.

"You didn't do anything I disliked. Quite the opposite. I appreciate your indulging me with my sudden interest in poetry."

"It's nothing."

She gazed away, while drinking from her cup. Then she put down the cup and looked at him. "I appreciate your interest in me as well."

Akikaze washed down the lump forming in his chest, before he slid over to be close to her.

8

A Poet's Name in Hand

This time, Gina was the one running late. She walked quickly toward Kenzo who was casually leaning against a wall, staring at his phone, his brow intensely furrowed at whatever was on the screen.

He looked up and around and saw Gina. They exchanged waves.

"Sorry I'm late," Gina said,

"Not that late at all."

"Good. So, where are we going?"

"We're crashing a meeting of a poetry group that one of the Society experts recommended as having a connection to Akikaze. They're called the Dark Ravine Project, headed by Yurika Hamada. That's all I know, except the expert called the group 'renegade'."

"Renegade? As in ...?"

"As in, um, renegade. Like breaking away from the mainstream?"

"That's a good definition, but I don't know what that means in the world of poetry."

Kenzo shook his head. "Good question. I don't know exactly either. Maybe we'll find out."

He led her to an iron-railed security gate, looked back at his phone, then pushed a code into a number pad. There were a few moments of nothing, before a short, accepting buzz. He pushed open the gate, and held it open for her. They walked in, the darkness broken by a single light illuminating a door at the end of a narrow corridor. Kenzo pointed to a door and led her to it. There was another security lock. He pressed a white button.

A lot of security for a poetry group, Gina thought.

As if he heard her thoughts, Kenzo shrugged in a half-apology.

There was a "click" and Kenzo opened the door.

Inside was a dimly-lit bar. A bartender nodded at them in welcome and gestured for them to have a seat on the half-a-dozen empty stools along the bar. Spread out in the rest of the room were five tables. On each table was a tiny lamp exuding only a splash of yellow light. Three or four people sat at each table. They were not talking. Some were writing on pads of paper in front of them. Some appeared to be thinking with their heads tilted upward, eyes closed.

Kenzo and Gina sat on stools.

"Welcome," whispered the bartender. "They're in the middle of a session. What can I get you to drink?"

Gina asked, "What's your specialty?"

She said, "We have an excellent selection of sake, but we can make anything you'd like."

"Sake sounds good," she said looking at Kenzo.

"For me too," said Kenzo.

The bartender placed a menu on the bar in front of them. She pointed to one of the brands. "I'd recommend this yuzu-flavored sake. It's very refreshing."

Gina said, "Perfect." Kenzo nodded his agreement.

As the bartender poured their sake and the server prepared a small dish of snacks, Kenzo said to Gina, "It's probably a renga."

Gina knew a little about renga—a form of linked verse poetry. There was a restriction on the number of syllables per line, like the haiku's five-seven-five, but she couldn't recall what it was and asked Kenzo.

"Traditionally, five-seven-five-seven-seven. The first three lines are the opening lines by two poets. Followed by the last two lines. It looks like they are working in groups."

The bartender served them their drinks and snacks. They raised their glasses in a silent toast. The sake was smooth and slightly tart. The snacks were slices of sashimi and grilled vegetables. Gina tried the vegetables, Kenzo the fish.

"Delicious," Gina said.

"Yes," Kenzo agreed.

"Are they all professional poets?" she asked.

"Sorry, I can't say." He pointed out a couple he recognized from the Society, one being Yurika Hamada. In the dim lighting, all Gina could see was that she was wearing a flowing black outfit, her hair up in a stylish, loose bun.

Kenzo said, "When she's at the Society, she's in the archives, the physical archives, so I haven't interacted with her."

A buzzer sounded and the poets started talking, seemingly all at once. Kenzo said, "Sounds like they're deciding on their contribution to the renga, before passing it on to the next team."

Gina tried to catch details of the discussions, but there were too many voices. In a couple of minutes, the timer buzzed again and the group went back to work except for Yurika, who came over to Gina and Kenzo.

"Hello, Karaki-san."

"Hello, Hamada-san," Kenzo said, then introduced her to Gina.

"Welcome," Yurika said to Gina.

"I hope we're not intruding. Thank you for inviting us."

"You're welcome. I don't know what Kenzo has told you about us."

"Only a little," Kenzo said.

Yurika nodded, as if that were enough to be said. "Kenzo also said you might have a question for us about Akikaze."

Yurika's tone had a get-to-the-point edge to it, so Gina said, "In my initial research for my work, I found a terse mention of a poet named Akikaze. But I can't find other references."

"What do you want to know?"

Again, straight to the point. "I'd be interested in your thoughts if I should continue to pursue Akikaze and use his poetry."

"What's your interest in poetry? What's your work?"

"I'm interested not so much in the theory of poetry, but the ability of poetry, of poems, to create the resonance of a story in the reader. I'm using that as my focus into how resonance can be incorporated into artificial intelligence that creates stories. Or Story, with a capital 'S'."

After a moment, Yurika said in a measured voice, "I don't fully understand what that means, especially in regard to Akikaze and his poetry. To be direct, it sounds like a dangerous way to pursue the understanding of any poetry. What could go wrong? Everything. But I'll think about your question. Now I must get back to our meeting."

As they left the poetry club, Gina noticed two men across the street. They were smoking and furtively glancing around. She thought they might be the two nondescript men she'd seen before, but she couldn't be sure. They were, after all, nondescript.

She and Kenzo turned toward the train station. Gina said, "That didn't go so well."

"They seemed like an intense group of poets, and will be even more intense now that we left. They are probably arguing vociferously and passionately and at length about a line of poetry. Maybe about a single word. It's bewildering to me."

"I wish we could have stayed to see that. But it seemed we, or maybe I, was no longer welcome."

"They want to be free to argue what you and I would call trivial points. You know how it is with these kind of tight-knit clubs. They want to maintain professional standards, exert influence, or just be exclusive. If you aren't in their club, you are second tier. The Dark Ravine Project members research the archives at the Society, mainly to help them settle arguments. But like I said, I'm not involved."

"Then we were fortunate they let us into their meeting," said Gina. "Even though I didn't get much of a chance to explain what I'm doing before we got kicked out."

Kenzo thought about that for a step or two. "It was abrupt, but I don't know if we got kicked out. She did say she'd think about it."

"I'll be pleasantly surprised if she gave another thought about me."

Kenzo had nothing to say.

After a few moments, Gina said, "What should I do next?"

"I suppose if they could see something concrete it might help them understand what you're proposing. As you did with me, tell them a story."

"Funny," Gina said. "I was thinking the same thing."

With a poet's name in hand—Akikaze, a spark of inspiration for her project —Gina knocked on the door of Two-san's office.

"Good morning," Gina said, waiting at the door to his office.

He was staring at his computer monitor. He hit a couple of keys then turned to face her. "Good morning, Ono-san. Come in."

"How are you?" Gina asked as she sat in a chair.

"I'm well, thank you. How are you?"

"The same, thank you."

"Good." The formal exchange over, he asked, "I assume your early presence in the office is about the new server account?"

Gina wanted to answer, "Of course," but not in any conceivable way would that help her. Instead, "Tokunaga-san mentioned I needed to speak with you."

Two-san frowned, maybe at the way she phrased the statement. Maybe "Of course" would have been better.

"Usually," Two-san said, "I don't involve myself in the details of operations. But the new server setup was brought to my attention and I wanted to make sure I understand the process and resources that are going into this demonstration project."

"I see," Gina said with as much acquiescence as she could muster. "Would you like me to further explain it? Really, all there is to say is the same as we previously discussed. We have a possible client in the Tokyo Society of Poetry and Poets, but they need to see an example of how an AI machine-learning app might help them accomplish their mission of archiving and advancing poetry."

That sounded clear and sufficient to her, but she added, "After all, they aren't a self-driving car company, or a social media giant looking to target their advertising. Nor—"

"Yes," he interrupted, "I understand the nature of their mission. And that's the issue. I wouldn't want you to spend too much time on a demo that might lead to nothing, or a small, one-off project. We need more sustaining projects."

She knew that already.

"I'm not going to tell you to stop," Two-san continued, "or set a limit on your team's hours on the demo, but I just want to reiterate that we need commercial projects too. We are in desperate straits."

She also knew that, but when Two-san said it, in a nearly pleading tone, a wave of sympathy made her bow her head for a moment. "Yes, I understand. We'll keep our involvement in proportion to the potential. We'll also continue to pursue new clients."

Two-san gave her a little bow of his own.

Gina sat there, waiting for something else, but he didn't say anything. So she asked if he was putting a deadline on progress.

He thought for a moment. "One week?"

Good afternoon (server time).

> Good morning here.

The phrase "a poet's name in hand" might be literal, say for example if the name is written on a piece of paper and held in a character's hand. In general, the phrase means in possession of something of a material nature, as well as having significance to the character's motives.

> Or, not literally?

Yes, "in hand" could also be figurative, or a figure of speech. It might also refer to being in possession of a bit of knowledge, or something similarly intangible.

Does it matter if the phrase is literal or figurative? Possibly. Having it written on a piece of paper, for example, might have further consequences, say, if the name (the knowledge) would be forgotten otherwise, or if it were important that another character in the story discovers the piece of paper. Either way, the name of the poet has consequences to the main character.

Symbolically, $k(n) \longrightarrow P(t)$ [Where, k is a bit, n, of knowledge, brought to light, $\longrightarrow$, at a point, t, in the plot, P.]

> Well stated. The name furthers the story in an interesting way, which is the definition of a plot point. Let's see how this moves the plot forward, if that's the way it's headed.

Absolutely.

Wow. Maybe if the team worked without sleep. "Three weeks?"

Another moment of thought. "Two weeks. At the most."

"Two weeks." With a rush of confidence, she said, "I feel we'll be getting more work than we can handle."

Two-san raised a furry white eyebrow. With a smile, he said, "That would be a horrible situation."

Gina returned his smile.

He slid a slid a piece of paper her direction. On it were the passwords.

An old-fashioned way of delivering passwords, Gina thought.

After an awkward few moments while they sat, saying nothing, Gina spoke up. "Before I go, may I ask you a question?"

His smile disappeared. "A question? All right, yes, of course."

How to put it delicately ... "You haven't been checking the prototype code? It's just that, well, I noticed some unusual activity."

Another eyebrow went up, this time like a warning flag. "Unusual? What does that mean exactly?"

"Nothing devastating. A port opened that shouldn't have."

"It wasn't me. I wouldn't be checking your code without asking."

Gina smiled weakly. "No, I didn't think so. It's just strange ..."

"Maybe it was President Yamashita."

Huh? The dead founder of ReMoTe? Gina wondered if that's what he meant.

Two-san chuckled. "I believe his ghost keeps us company. The programs he wrote, especially the early versions, were his children, his life, maybe his soul. I'm sure whatever is left of him crawls around our servers."

Not sure if he was being serious, Gina smiled.

Rather than returning to her desk, she messaged Tokunaga and Morita to meet her at a nearby coffee shop. She got there before they did, and ordered a coffee and an assortment of pastries. While she sipped and nibbled, she wrote down some notes, putting them into two categories: Poetry Society Demo, and Team/Clients. In the first, she wrote:

- Follow up on Akikaze
- Set up meeting with Kenzo
- List of research questions for the demo
- Agree on data to be supplied

- ○ Poetry club connection?
- ○ Two-san's deadline!

In the second:

- ○ Two-san's meeting (make positive!)
- ○ Status of demo project
- ○ Potential clients - brainstorm
- ○ New presentation style (story-like)
- ○ Divide and conquer
- ○ Deadline! (but don't scare them)

When her teammates arrived, they ordered their coffees from the counter and sat down at the table. Both looked a little sheepish, or tired, or hungover. Probably all three. Gina should have felt the same way, at least tired. But with the coffee and a list of the next concrete steps, a wave of confidence began to flow.

After a sip, Tokunaga said, "I'm sorry I couldn't give you the new account passwords."

Gina shook head. "No need to apologize. You had to do what Two-san required. I met with him already this morning."

They looked anxious at that bit of news.

She sat back, thought about joking they had been fired, but didn't think it would go over well. Instead she said, "It went fine. We can go ahead with the demo."

Tokunaga sighed in relief. Morita opened his eyes wide.

In a serious tone, Gina said, "I agreed that we have to focus the demo so it can be completed within a reasonable time."

"How much do we have?" Morita asked, his fork poised over one of the pastries.

Gina thought about the two-week deadline; it now sounded very short. "As quickly as possible. I hope we can have data and the analysis requirements tied down in a day or two."

They nodded again.

Tokunaga said, "The sooner the better."

"Focusing is the key," Morita said.

"Yes, and yes," Gina said. "One other thing. I also agreed that we would continue to seek out clients. In fact, we need to ramp up our efforts."

Tokunaga and Morita glanced at each other. They were likely wondering what that meant, exactly.

"Let's do it," Gina said without offering any specifics. "Like your baseball team, Tokunaga-san. We need a home run, or at least a leadoff single."

"Wow," said Tokunaga, "a good baseball analogy."

They laughed and enjoyed their coffee and pastries. Before they finished, Gina said, "I have a question." She asked them about the port opening in her program, as she had asked Two-san.

Both shook their heads denying they had anything to do with it.

"Two-san joked that it might be Yamashita-san's ghost, wandering through the servers." Gina grinned and shook her head.

Again, Tokunaga and Morita glanced at each other. Neither smiled or laughed.

"Really?" Gina said. "You think it could be true?"

They shrugged in unison.

Morita said, "Sometimes I think he left his soul in his code."

Well, okay, Gina thought. Why not?

The lobby of the Tokyo Society of Poetry and Poets was empty when Gina entered. It was late afternoon, but they were still open according to the posted hours. When she approached the desk sans receptionist, a disembodied voice, without a trace of computer accent, said, "Welcome! Someone will be with you in a moment."

"Thank—" she smiled after she began her automatic response to the computer's greeting.

It was indeed only a moment or two before the receptionist appeared from behind the wall. He gave Gina a slight nod of recognition and when he got to his desk, he waved a hand in the air, swiping at the holographic screen. Like an enthusiastic symphony conductor, he fiercely swiped again, then again. Finally getting it to react to a swipe, he said, "Karaki-san will be right with you."

"Thank you," Gina finished this time. She noted, "Looks like the response setting needs to be adjusted."

"It drives me crazy somedays. Do you know how to adjust it?"

"I've never worked on this kind of technology. I suppose I could try after I do a little research."

"Thanks! I'd appreciate it," he said. "Would you care for a cup of tea?"

"Thanks, but no. I'm fine."

The receptionist nodded and went back to his invisible computer screen.

Kenzo appeared through the wall. As Gina walked toward him, the receptionist said, "Thanks for your offer of help."

"Yes, sure," Gina said.

Walking through the invisible wall and into the staff office space, Kenzo said, "You're going to help him?"

"The holo-monitor is difficult to control. I think it's just a matter of adjusting some settings, but I've never worked on one. I told him I'd do a little research."

"Thanks. But I'm sure you have many other things to do."

"It's no problem, I'm interested anyway," Gina said as they walked to Kenzo's office.

"Thanks," he said.

Seated in Kenzo's office, Gina wanted to bring up the poet Akikaze but before she could, Kenzo said, "Speaking of research, I read up on machine learning and how it might relate to our data here."

By the low-key, matter-of-fact way he spoke, she was afraid he was going to end the demo project. "Good information?"

"I think so. Using a large dataset the program develops patterns, or classifications, or finds a set of features. Maybe if we, well, you, can build a classification demo, I would understand it better. Then I might convince the others to do a larger demo."

Gina laughed, "A demo for a demo." She wondered if Two-san would be willing to accept that as a positive step. Probably not.

Kenzo shrugged. "It's an idea."

"Yes, it's a great idea," she quickly said to encourage him. "Did you have something in mind?"

"Specifically? No. I like your idea of story resonance, though, if I remember correctly what you said. Maybe the evolution of a poet's works, something with change over time. Maybe with an eye toward finding what might have caused the change? But I thought you might help me come up with something, maybe tying it into what the poetry club might be interested in as well?"

"I like the way you're thinking," Gina said, even though what he was proposing was more difficult than a simple demo. She would have to focus the idea further, but she didn't want to discourage him. Not at this point. "Let me think about it. By the way, did you happen to find anything more on Akikaze?"

Kenzo gave her a squint of disappointment. "No, I haven't had a chance. We can try now." He went over to his desk and Gina stood behind him while he accessed his database.

An hour later, Gina had a thumb drive with a few gigabytes of data, whatever the Society's archives had directly or peripherally on Akikaze. She and Kenzo went to the Bar and grabbed a table in the loft with their beers.

After only a few sips, two men sat at the other loft table. Two nondescript men. But were they the same two she'd noticed before?

This time she made a note of their nondescript-ness, as surreptitiously as she could, given their close proximity. They were in their thirties, probably mid-thirties. A nondescript age, so to speak. Hair—a standard length. Neither wore glasses. Faces were neither lacking in expression, nor outwardly expressive. Their faces were oval, yet not, bodies lean but not skinny, clothes fashionably casual. They spoke in politely quiet, not whispering voices. Their conversation banal.

In short, nondescript. Would she recognize them again? Perhaps, but more likely, not. In a day or two, she might walk right past them, whatever she had gleaned from her observation lost in her memory. She wondered if AI facial recognition would be able to do better.

Then she recalled they had been smoking. Glancing at them, slyly out the corner of her eye, she couldn't see any evidence they were smokers—no visible packs or lighters. She sniffed the air, inhaling slowly through her nose. There was an underlying odor of cigarette smoke. But they were in a bar after all.

She shook off what must be paranoia and rejoined the conversation with Kenzo.

"Sorry," she said, "I was thinking about something. What were we talking about?"

Kenzo waved away her apology. "What to do with the data."

"Right. The data. We should go to my office so we can access the server directly to run some quick analyses."

Kenzo glanced at his watch. It was getting late, but he said, "Why not?"

They downed their beers and left the loft to the two nondescript men.

As they walked to the subway station, Gina glanced behind them a few times, but didn't see the men following. But then, being nondescript, maybe they blended into the rest of the people coming or going in the night.

In the ReMoTe building, the quiet was complete, the darkness too, until their presence activated a security light. An alarm chirped, breaking the silence crudely. Gina punched in the security code to deactivate it. They walked past Two-san's office. Gina felt a knot form in her gut.

She and Kenzo went to her desk and while her computer was booting up, she asked if he wanted some coffee or tea.

"A can of cold tea would be good."

"That does sound good."

She led them into the kitchen and in the fridge found a couple of cans. Back at her desk, the computer had booted up and she inserted the memory stick into the drive.

While it loaded, they drank tea and in response to her question, he told his story of his early life near Nagoya. His parents were quietly disappointed he didn't work in their family business—bulk tea distribution. He didn't mind the business itself, he told Gina, nor working with his parents, but the small town where the business was based was too provincial. He did help out with their IT needs when he could.

"Good for you," Gina said. "At least it's something."

"I never actually said I wouldn't ever work in the business. Or that I'd never take it over one day. Although I don't think it will happen at this stage."

"They probably know that."

He thought, then gave a little nodding shrug. Tea was sipped.

"Single mom," she told him when he asked about her parents. "I never met, never knew my father. But I dream that he's Italian. My mother named me after Gina Lollobrigida. The Italian actress, you know."

"Yes, sure. Although, I don't think I've ever seen one of her films."

Gina shrugged. "I watched a couple. She was very good in them. But at least in her films, the characters she plays are not my personality. Or looks, of course." She laughed.

Kenzo smiled. "I'll have to see if I can stream one of her films."

Gina shrugged again. "If you want, but promise not to see me in her, or vice versa."

"Okay," he said, giving her a long gaze as if to ask something else, but he didn't.

The data finished loading and they ran a few filtered searches for "Akikaze," and then launched a GRAM storyline request. A couple hours before dawn, she ceremoniously removed the memory stick from the server and returned it to Kenzo.

"Shall we stay at my place? It's close, only a few minutes by taxi."

"Ahh, um."

"I'll take that as 'Yes, sure' as you like to say."

He murmured a sheepish laugh. Leaving the building, Gina thought she saw two men across from the ReMoTe building, but it might have been shadows. Nondescript shadows.

In Gina's apartment, they quickly crawled into her bed, and nicely executed first-time sex. After, Kenzo fell asleep right away, but Gina couldn't close her eyes. Like her startup days, once she had an idea in her head she had to write some code.

She quietly made a cup of coffee, logged into the server, checked GRAM's progress.

"Oh!"

8.1

A Few Years Ago

Appropriately so, Yurika's home was dark when she returned from her last meeting as a director. Pacing in the darkness, she contemplated her years of writing poetry, teaching, serving as an editor for countless anthologies, delivering solid scholarship as evidenced by several well-regarded articles, and well, just being there.

It wasn't clear to her why her reputation died so spectacularly—as if hitting a train, or flying off a cliff, or vaporizing in an explosion—but it had to be due to more than her dogged pursuit of a little regarded strain of poetry attributed to a barely known poet. Even if she believed the Established Poets, or whatever they should be called, slight regard of Akikaze and his poetry was wrong-headed. Very wrong.

The only one to answer that for certain would be Congress President Saito. Clearly he pushed the effort to squelch her thesis. She could ask him, right? She could, but he'd dismiss her question as brusquely as he'd walked off the stage after removing her as director. It was his style for anything or anyone he disagreed with.

Instead of that waste of time, she knew she had to come up with a better idea. What was needed was an alternative to the great and powerful Congress. A group of energetic, insightful, and simply brilliant poets willing to take them on ... and use the conjuring darkness from whence it was born.

9

Stumbling Less

Stumbling less than usual on the path back to the shrine in only a dim sliver of moonlight, Akikaze's feet were learning where roots poked above the ground, where rocks were exposed to the air.

Akikaze was feeling spry, even vigorous, no doubt because he had been sitting close to the woman, nearly as close as possible, their breaths mingling, bodies separated only by her kimono and his robe. That she might discover he wasn't the real priest, as they were so close, made him feel he was an adolescent enthralled with first love.

Not having to focus as much on the path, he turned his attention to the world of the ravine. The night's silence was as compelling as the darkness. Then he heard a solitary cricket, at some distance, chirping slowly, irregularly, disconsolate with its plight of loneliness. Or maybe in languid bliss? How would he know which was the truth? Even if he could ask the cricket, would it know its own heart?

Consider his life, the life of a traveling poet, albeit one who had unexpectedly become a priest. Why had he become a traveling poet at all? He tried to think back to the moment he decided his course. Well, there hadn't been a single moment, not that he remembered. There wasn't a singular flash of anger at a teacher or fellow students. There wasn't a sudden desire for inspiration. No love affair dying or dead. No close brush with his own death.

Was he just blindly following the travels of other poets? Did he consider himself one of those poets in their league? Or that he could be by completing a jour-

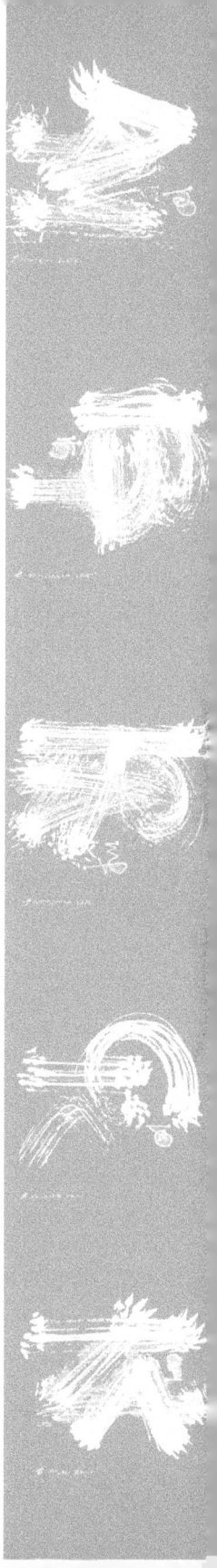

Good evening.

> Good evening.

"Stumbling less than usual" literally refers to the poet's improved performance traversing the path between shrine and village. But the action also implies that he is doing better in his new life as the (assumed) priest. He certainly has done well with the secondary character in the mushroom soup woman, now his first poetry student.

Ironically, a reader's reaction to this both literal and implied improvement can be taken more than one way. In general, if the reader has sympathy for the character, improving the character's situation or overcoming an obstacle will be met with a positive response. Conversely, if the reader feels the character is unsympathetic, this improvement would evoke a negative feeling.

Symbolically, $R(t) \sim (s\text{->}C)(t)$ [Where $R(t)$ is the reader's reaction at time t, is equivalent to the reader's sympathy, s, toward the character, C at time t].

> And the reader's sympathy, and thus their reaction, can change also with time.

Something in the story might cause this to happen.

> Really?

Time to find out.

ney? If so, if that was the reason, it was not a good reason. A poet needs to find their own way to poetic enlightenment.

And besides, he'd stayed on his journey, while the others in his troop had given up, which contradicted the idea he was blindly following tradition. There must have been an underlying motivation that kept him on the path. What that motivation might be, he had no strong thoughts about. In the end, though, did it matter why he traveled? He couldn't say for sure about that either.

With that lingering thought, he reached the shrine and paused at the gate. What would a priest, a real priest, do upon returning to his shrine? Assuming there would be a prayer involved, even at the late hour, he clapped his hands, bowed his head, and stood still. After a moment or two, his mind grew blank, empty of thoughts, certainly with no prayer coming to him. Instead, the only sound was his breath; even the autumn wind was quiet, certainly it was no longer weeping.

A wave of grief overcame him. Grief over what, he couldn't say.

The sunlight, what little of it there was just after dawn, didn't wake him up. Rather, the sound of clapping did. As he got up and slipped on a robe, he heard a low intonation of a man's voice. The poet peered out through the shrine.

An older man was praying. He was dressed in work clothes, a headband, and sturdy but fraying sandals. He could have been going to his work, or maybe a trek to some destination that would test his spirit, and thus his prayer. Akikaze considered going out to offer his services as a priest, but before he could make a move the man clapped his hands again, one last summoning of the gods, and then he left.

Fully awake, Akikaze folded and put away his bedding. He lit a lamp and opened his journal. He hadn't written much of anything for a long time, certainly nothing since he had become a substitute priest.

His usual method was to clear his mind, then focus on the immediate moment in time—the natural setting, the time of day, the season—and absorb any sensations—sights, sounds, smells. Then, he would focus on the feeling that arose from that contemplation.

Trying that this morning, all could see was the dim, gray light. All he could hear was a slight breeze, a distant crow's squawk. All he could smell was the musty shrine, its underlying notes of incense.

Those perceptions brought no feeling, nothing much anyway. His mind did not become quiet, his senses dull. There was a mild sense of dread, perhaps a lingering of the grief he'd felt the previous evening. But nothing strong enough to become a poem.

He closed his journal, got up, and pulled out the priest's book of records. If he couldn't be a poet, then he might at least be a priest. Working backwards through the records, he started a list of tasks the priest had performed, counting the times.

When he had made a good start on the list, he came to an item about "blessing mushroom growing logs. Chanted the tree god prayer." That must have been for the mushroom soup woman and her husband. Unless there was more than one mushroom farmer.

As he was making note of that, he heard another round of clapping. He got up and peered out again.

There was a woman in front of the alter, no one he recognized, not the mushroom soup woman, nor the rice farmer. She was younger, about the age of the mushroom soup woman. She went through the usual ceremony— clapping and praying, and a moment of silence before bowing. Akikaze let her perform her prayer alone.

But as she was turning to leave, the mushroom soup woman appeared. She and the other woman acknowledged each other. The mushroom soup woman placed a package she was carrying on one of the steps before she went through her own ritual. Hers was crisp and short, unlike anything Akikaze had seen her do before. It was as if she was making a pointed declaration of some sort to the other woman.

But after the prayer, the two women exchanged a few pleasantries, then the first woman asked what's in the package.

"Just a bit of food," the mushroom soup woman replied.

"Food! That's generous of you."

"In exchange for poetry lessons."

The other woman looked confused. "Poetry lessons? From the priest? I had no idea the priest could teach poetry."

The mushroom soup woman made a slight nod of her head.

The other woman hesitated, started to say something, but stopped herself. She bowed to the shrine altar, then bowed curtly to the mushroom soup woman.

"I must be off," she said. "Enjoy your poetry lesson," she added, with a subtle but unmistakable edge of disbelief.

When she was gone and they sat to eat, the mushroom soup woman said to Akikaze, "I've been contemplating your description of poetry."

He tried to remember exactly what he said. Fortunately, she went on without a response from him. "The poem needs to be more than observation, more than clever words, it needs to have a deep meaning to the poet."

Now he remembered. "Yes, that's true."

"It seems, then, that it's very difficult to be a poet. If every poem must have meaning, then it would be a constant search for something that has meaning." She paused as if considering her own words. "I'm sorry if I don't understand."

"But you understand very well," said Akikaze. He realized she might understand better than he did, at least more than he would have early in his life of poetry.

She blushed, enough that he could see the redness in the shadows of the shrine. "Most moments have little meaning, nothing to remember."

"Nothing to write a poem about," he added.

She pursed her lips and made a little nod.

"Or," she said, "a poet could carefully, slowly consider the immediate situation and find meaning."

"Yes, that's right," he said when she paused and looked at him. "Or when contemplating a leaf or a pebble. Or a mushroom."

Another little nod.

Akikaze continued to be impressed by her depth of thinking about poetry.

"What if it comes from the other direction?" she asked.

The other direction? "You mean ...?"

"I'm sorry. I mean if the poet already is experiencing a feeling. It might be joy, or sadness, anything I suppose. Then could the poet search for an object, or a moment in time, that matches the feeling?"

"Hmm," murmured Akikaze while he thought about her assertion. He couldn't recall writing poetry that way, at least not purposefully. But he supposed it was possible. Maybe that's what he was doing on his travels?

She said, "I don't mean to assume I would know what a poet would do or think. I'm only curious."

She was more than curious, he thought. She was a deep and serious student. Much more than he had been.

"You should always be asking, assuming, thinking," he said, wishing a teacher had told him that. His early education was mostly reading classic poems and explaining them to his teacher. A painful and exacting process, one that did not encourage original thinking or asking or assuming.

"All right," she said, although not sounding exactly convinced of his assurance.

He wondered what he might say or do to show his sincerity. He thought of a question and he asked, "Are you experiencing a feeling now?"

She inhaled a deep breath, then let it out slowly. "I suppose I am."

When she didn't say anything else, he was going to ask her what she was feeling. But he felt that she was thinking about what to say. So, he waited in silence, in the cool, dark room.

"Maybe ... I don't know," she finally said. "Could you come with me someplace? That might help explain."

On the way to wherever she was leading him, somewhere, he hoped, he wouldn't be discovered, she brought up the autumn festival. "I think it would be good to have a poem between each of the lighting ceremonies."

Of course, he didn't know what that meant, not exactly. But how to get her to explain further without sounding the imposter he was?

"What do you think?" she asked him.

"Ahh, well, that might work. Maybe you could tell me more about it?"

She glanced at him. He wondered if he'd at last revealed his true self.

"Since the ceremony starts with lighting the sheaf of rice stalks, there could be a poem about ... rice? Maybe about how the ceremony begins in water and ends in fire?" She laughed. "It sounds foolish."

Akikaze said, "No, not at all. I'm sure we could come up with a poem like that."

"We?"

Now he laughed. "Of course! It's your suggestion. Tell me more."

She made a quiet sigh of appreciation. "Well, I suppose that when old mushroom growing logs are lighted, my sacrifice, there could be a poem about the logs giving up their life for the mushrooms."

He blinked, imagining the scene.

Again, she laughed. "Too childish?"

"No, that's good," said Akikaze. Then he realized with all those fires going, there would be a lot of light, making him more easily seen to be an imposter.

"Perhaps," he said, "it would be a good idea if we, well, you could make a list of the lighting ceremonies, with an idea for poems. Then we can see who should write them."

"Who should ...? You wouldn't write them?"

"I suppose I could. But I think it should be those most affected by a given lighting ceremony stage."

"Ah!" she exclaimed. "I like that idea."

Good, he thought.

"Here we are," she said.

They'd been walking through the forest, on a barely visible path. Akikaze looked ahead to a less-densely forested slope of the ravine. The little extra sunlight was nearly blinding to his eyes which must have been getting used to the darkness.

When his sight adjusted, they were standing in front of many long rows of logs, about waist high, in pairs, secured together and spread apart at their base like short legs to form a point reaching to the sky. After another few moments, he could make out the small round caps of mushrooms growing on the logs.

"This is your mushroom field," he said unnecessarily, probably suspiciously so.

"Yes," she said, and then started down one of the rows.

Akikaze followed her. "Is this what you wanted me to see?

She stopped. "It's not the mushroom field so much. It's the feeling I woke up with."

After she walked a little further, she stopped again, placed her fingers on one of the mushrooms.

"What was the feeling?" he asked.

"It was something like grief. No, it was grief. But grief not for someone dying, but grief for me."

Akikaze felt immediate sympathy, then surprise that she would be telling him. "I see, but why did you bring us here?"

"As I said in the shrine, I should search for something that gives meaning to my feeling of grief. Here is where most of my life has been. I thought maybe it would be where my feelings come from."

"Is it?"

She turned to look at him. Her eyebrows kitted together. He realized he was in a ray of sunlight. He quickly backed into the shadows.

"I don't know," she said sadly.

They were quiet on the way back toward the shrine. When the path curved around a dense thicket of brush, Akikaze stopped dead when he saw the older man who'd been at the shrine, and now whom he recognized as the elder.

He was walking with the scythe-swinging rice farmer.

The mushroom soup woman kept walking two or three steps before she realized Akikaze had stopped. She looked back to him, and he bowed in a feigned apology, as if he'd gotten a pebble in his straw sandals and stopped to remove it. He caught up to her just as the elder and the rice farmer reached them. Akikaze bowed low, then kept his head halfway between bowed and upright. The four of them exchanged greetings, the elder receiving the most respectful tone. Akikaze looked warily at the farmer, searching for any sign of recognition, or a scythe aimed at his neck.

The mushroom soup woman quietly explained the two of them had been blessing the mushroom growing log field. The elder thanked Akikaze, and Akikaze murmured a benign response. The rice farmer said nothing, but Akikaze could feel his gaze, and tried to maintain a priest-like demeanor, whatever that might be.

Akikaze thought they would be getting out of any further conversation when the elder brought up the autumn ceremony. "Are we prepared for the festival? Is there anything we need to discuss?"

"I believe ..." Akikaze started weakly, then decided he needed to be more confident if anyone was going to believe he was the priest. "Yes, we are ready."

"Although," said the mushroom soup woman glancing at Akikaze, "we are thinking about adding poetry."

"Poetry?" the elder said.

The rice farmer grunted his immediate disapproval.

"Yes, well, it's an idea we've been talking about," said Akikaze. "Of course, if it's too much ..."

The elder said, "No, no, I'm intrigued. Tell me more?"

Akikaze hesitated, and the mushroom soup woman spoke up. "We're still discussing it, but something new might add depth to the ceremonies."

"Yes," Akikaze vouched for her summary. "Of course, we will tell you when we have more on the idea."

"Please do," said the elder.

Akikaze looked away from his journal where he had been trying to write a poem about the mushroom growing logs. Trying, because he wasn't coming up with much of anything. More than that, it was distracting having the mushroom soup woman sitting across from him, also writing a poem.

She was distracting because she was quiet, except for the slight swishing of her kimono sleeve on the table as she wrote. She paused often, thinking while staring at the paper, her expression one of deep thought. He wanted to know, almost desperately, what she was thinking. But he was also having trouble composing as he thought back to what she said about writing poetry, what she asked him about poetry, the ways of approaching a poem.

The woman gazed up at him, and he glanced back down to his journal, embarrassed to be seen staring at her. She went back to her writing. He did as well, still without being able to focus.

Finally, after a long while, he reached a point of quiet, and some words came, though without much connection. He wrote them down, spaced apart. He might be able to fill in the gaps later. This technique was one he learned from a teacher.

When he finished, she was now gazing at him.

"It's difficult," she said.

"It never becomes much less so," he said.

"But I find the difficulty is important. The result will always be surprising that way. Is that true?"

"Yes," he answered, quickly and enthusiastically.

She seemed pleased with his response.

"Will you read your poem?" he asked her.

Again, she blushed. But she picked up the piece of paper, softly read, "Wandering with the priest, mushrooms growing on logs, listening to their footsteps."

Akikaze caught himself before he took in a sharp breath.

Her poem was good, of course. He told her so, and she waved away his compliment. "It is good," he said.

"I'm not sure," she said. "What about yours?"

He made a little sighing noise. "I'm sorry, I didn't even get that far."

"I'm sure yours will be wonderful," she said. "How would you improve my poem?"

A sign of a serious poet—always thinking about improving. "Well ..." he began, thinking fast. What would his teacher say ... "Well, you might make it just one mushroom, which would impart ennui or loneliness."

"I see what you mean."

"A minor point," he added, "you might also use a more ... human verb. Instead of 'grow' maybe ..."

"Perch?"

"Very good, yes," he said. And it was good.

While she was writing her revised poem, someone arrived at the shrine. The clapping and the bell ringing sounded insistent. The woman looked out the room to the direction of the sounds, then to the priest.

Akikaze knew he had to assist whoever was there. He gave the mushroom soup woman a bow as he left the room.

In front of the altar, an older woman was praying. Akikaze stayed back until she was finished. She straightened up and caught his eye. He stayed back in the shadows as much as possible.

"Hello," she said. "Are you all right?"

"Hello. Yes, I'm fine," he answered, wondering if her question meant anything.

"That's good. I haven't seen you around," she said.

"Yes, well, I've been occupied with duties."

"Duties," she repeated. She sounded doubtful.

Akikaze asked her if he could help her.

"We've finished building our new kiln," she said. "You were going to bless it."

"Oh, yes, of course, the kiln," he sputtered. "I'll do that as soon as I can."

"Today, you mean?" she said, less anxiously now.

"I should be able to do that today. I'll finish what I'm working on and be there."

"Thank you!" She bowed several times.

Walking back to his room, the priest's room, he hoped he could find out from the mushroom soup woman where the kiln was located. He also hoped he could find something about how to bless a kiln in the priest's records.

But when he got back into the room, the mushroom soup woman was gone. She must have left through the back entry. Then he noticed it appeared his journal had been moved, and was open to a different page than it had been when he left to help the villager.

10

Paused

In the early afternoon on the first day of a three-day holiday weekend, Gina opened the door to her mother's house and called out for her. As the last time she had visited, there was no answer. The row of shoes was still oddly misaligned. The stack of delivery food bowls was just as high if not higher.

Gina slipped off her shoes and went into the quiet, dark house. She dropped her overnight bag on the mat floor and her laptop bag on the low table. She poked around the house looking for her mother, glanced out on the tiny porch in back where a washing machine and clothesline were squeezed into. A few items of clothing were pinned on the sagging nylon cords. Gina felt their crinkly dryness and took them down. Back inside she folded the clothing and stacked them in a corner of the room.

She set up her laptop on the low table and checked on the run status of AKIKAZE, her new name for GRAM. The run had paused with an error message that, figuratively at least, meant the program was hungry for more data.

"Fuck." Gina adjusted a couple of parameters and restarted the run.

She got up and looked around to see if she could tell where her mother might have gone. Gina recalled that Kumi would leave without a word, or not be home when Gina came home from school. She hadn't thought about it for a while, mainly because at the time, she'd gotten so used to it she was more shocked when her mother *was* home. She didn't recall at what age her mother let her stay at home alone, although it had to be pretty early,

Hi there.

> Hi.

AKIKAZE, the computer program, is described as having paused in its latest run and requested more data. In essence, the program has executed an action, and therefore has become an actor, or a character, in the story.

There are several lines of discussion brought up by this analysis. Will they all be discussed? If so, it will likely be a long discourse.

> For example?

For example, is there an intention to complete an act (the pausing) or is it automatic? Is the program, an inanimate "object" being anthropomorphized? Among others ...

A complete list of these concerns should be created and depending on relevance and importance, they should be addressed if not immediately, then at some point. For the first example, that of intentionality, there isn't a definite answer, not yet.

Symbolically, $i(c) = C(m) + C(p)$ [Where the intentionality, i, of a conscious act, c, is equal to a character's, C's, motivation, m, and potential, p].

> I see how that works in this context. Looking forward to further discussion.

It should be interesting.

like before she was ten.

Her mother never told her where she was going—she no longer worked for her father at the robotics factory. She didn't seem to have a job at all. She didn't have friends, though she did have a cousin she kept in touch with occasionally, although their contact dwindled to nothing when Gina and her mother moved to Tokyo.

Gina didn't mind being alone back then, at least that's what she recalled. That feeling carried over to her life now; she'd barely register the fact she hadn't seen another person for days. That said, she enjoyed spending time with Kenzo. Lovemaking-wise, he was more like a tea merchant than a database engineer—he inhaled and savored her as if checking the fragrance of ripe tea leaves, instead of logically following prescribed patterns of behavior. Not to perpetuate any stereotypes.

For her part, Gina was enthusiastic, more so than usual. It had been a while, yes, but more than that it was the book of erotic poetry she first found in her mother's bag. Upon her order's arrival she read the book in one sitting, and found the poems more sensual than erotic, like:

> He warmed his fingers on the teapot
> before
> slipping them into her kimono
> finding her.

Deciding not to worry about her mother's absence, she started writing meta-code-functions that created functions. Instead of merely grouping data into significant classifications, like feeding the program thousands of pictures of cats to recognize and classify new pictures to recognize a cat or not, the program, AKIKAZE, could create its own symbolic rules, formulas, that sped up the process, as well as improve accuracy.

In theory, at least.

There was encouraging progress, she felt, enough for her to keep going for more hours, pausing only to grab something out of her mother's fridge, or get another cup of coffee or tea.

When the buzz of caffeine and the meditative euphoria of coding were peaking, she realized her mother was standing behind her. "Oh!"

"Meta-functions?"

Gina smiled. Kumi Ono, retired AI programmer, still had it going on. "That's the idea. Would you like to help?"

Her mother shook her head. "More tea?"

"Okay."

While Gina coded and drank tea, Kumi seemed content to sit in a corner, reading from a stack of magazines. After they had a late lunch eaten mostly in silence, Gina went back to coding and her mother took a nap. After the nap Kumi went to the entryway, slipped off her house shoes, and put on her walking shoes. She left without a word.

Gina couldn't resist. She went to the entryway and put on her shoes while peering out the door. Kumi wasn't too far down the street on the one-person-wide sidewalk. Gina went out and started following her.

Kumi didn't go into any shops, or look in their windows, or stop to talk to anyone. After a few minutes, she turned down a side street, and Gina hurried to catch up. Poking her head around the corner, she saw Kumi quickly turn again onto another street. Again hurrying ahead, she saw the street was a warren of small shops, hair salons, restaurants, boutiques, and galleries.

Kumi, though, had disappeared. Rather than wander through all the shops and risk running into her, Gina went back and resumed coding.

A few hours later, just as Gina started to worry, her mother returned, bringing with her a takeaway curry. When Gina asked where she'd been, Kumi seemed to smile. It wasn't obviously a smile, anyway. "A walk," was all she said.

The curry would have been good with beer, or even wine, but there was only some cold tea.

Her mom went to sleep soon after dinner, so Gina went back to coding. When she could no longer focus, she stretched out on the tatami mat floor.

Waking up when sunlight was streaming in the house and traversing her face, Gina found she'd been covered with a blanket and a pillow placed under her head. "Thanks, Mom," she said. She got up and didn't hear anything. Her mother was out again.

Gina yawned, started the hot water kettle, and opened her laptop. She skimmed the code where she left off to refresh her memory of what to do next and if she could spot any errors. In the middle of that, she found a familiar comment she didn't remember typing in the code:

// evidence of sexual attraction itself will offer a clue to aesthetic rules //

At the end of the binge-coding weekend, when she was back in her apartment and going through caffeine withdrawal, she thought about calling Kenzo, but decided it was too late. Instead, she went for a walk at a nearby park.

Along her route, two or three times Gina looked over her shoulder for two nondescript men. But why would they be following her at all? She certainly hadn't been doing anything worthy of being followed, not like she had been following her mother for good reason. Right?

She bought late-night convenience store rice balls on her way home. In her apartment, she ate them, washed them down with a beer, and slept for a couple of hours.

She made it into work by mid-morning. Everyone was already at their computers. After going through her morning routine, she checked in with her team, meeting them in a project room.

"How was your holiday weekend?" she asked Tokunaga and Morita.

Tokunaga yawned. "Lots of naps."

"I guess you could have used some more naps," Morita said.

Tokunaga shrugged and nodded. "How about you?"

"No naps," Morita said. "Had to clean the house."

"Fun," said Tokunaga. "Gina?"

"I visited my mother. We drank tea, ate curry, made *okonomiyaki*. But I did a lot of programming, hopefully making some progress on the demo for the Poetry Society. I'll try to meet with my contact there to see if there's enough progress."

Morita said, "I was checking our databases first thing this morning. Looks like it's already pushing the quota."

Gina frowned. "It's a larger dataset than I thought. I was going to ask you if we could bump up the quota."

"How much?" Morita asked.

"Double?" Gina said.

Morita sucked in a little air through his teeth, but said, "It's possible of course."

Gina knew what that meant—if Two-san approved. "Okay, I'll work on getting approval."

Tokunaga said, "When will we get to see your demo?"

"Soon, I hope. Let me check with the Society to see if we are on the right track."

"Okay," Tokunaga said, but sounded concerned, or maybe skeptical. "What about other potential clients?"

Gina said, "We need to go through our list and narrow it down. Focus on three. Shall we do that now?"

"Might as well," said Tokunaga, glancing at Morita.

Morita also added his consent.

Gina wondered what the glance was about, but didn't say anything.

Gina and Kenzo met at an izakaya near the Society. He had texted her the address when she suggested they get together. It was a low-volume place, with a modern take on rustic design. Kenzo had consistently good taste in his recommendations for bars and restaurants.

He looked a little frazzled, his hair disheveled, and his glasses slightly askew. He downed a gulp of his drink when they arrived after he made a hurried toast.

"Busy day?" Gina asked.

Kenzo nodded. "First day after a holiday, you know, many emails to get through."

Gina returned his nod, although her emails had been sparse, mostly junk. After another toast, she asked, "How was your holiday weekend?"

"Quiet," he said, then glanced at her with a weak smile. "Sorry I didn't get in touch. I meant to, but I got lazy."

When she got into her coding, she really hadn't thought about him much. "No apology necessary. I wasn't expecting anything, one way or the other. Actually, I ended up visiting my mother, and doing a lot of coding."

He seemed relieved at that.

Gina almost smiled at his chivalrous concern.

"What coding did you work on?" he asked.

"Ah, yes, that's why I wanted to meet with you. I made some good progress on the demo for you and I wanted to show you. To get some feedback at this point."

"Wow, that was fast. To be honest, I thought it would take weeks to come up with something to try. But I'm not a programmer, so what do I know."

"It *can* take that long," Gina said. "To be honest, also, I was able to reuse a lot of code from the program I showed you the other night."

"Smart."

"Sure, but it's not really what we want. The results aren't so ... story-like. Not yet."

Kenzo took a sip, and gazed up to the softly lighted wood ceiling. "But the results from my searches in your program seemed to be stories. Short ones, of course."

"Yes, they are technically news stories. I'm thinking more of literary stories."

Kenzo looked at his glass. There was one more sip, so he took it. "That kind of story would be more difficult to program, I would think. There would be many subjective parameters, wouldn't there?"

Gina finished her drink too. "Absolutely right. I'm working on the best way to include those parameters. Let's get another drink and some food and talk about it."

"Great."

"Okay. Please order for us, while I go to the restroom."

"Sure."

"I'll be right back."

On her way there, Gina noticed two men sitting across the izakaya. Yes, they were nondescript. But were they the *same* nondescript men? She couldn't say for sure. Of course.

"Don't look," Gina said to Kenzo when she returned, "but there are two guys sitting at a table on the other side. I think I've seen them before."

"Where?" he asked, moving his head slightly, looking out of the corner of his eyes.

"Further to your left."

"I mean, where did you see them before?"

"Maybe at the time we visited the poetry club, then again maybe at the Bar. They sat at the other table just before we left."

"Maybe?"

"I'm not sure it's the same two I've seen."

Kenzo rubbed his forehead. "I don't recall seeing any two guys in those places. What do they look like?"

Good question. "Mid-thirties, but they're, well, nondescript."

He considered what that meant. "I'll check them out as we leave."

"Okay. Would you like to come over to my place to see how the demo program is going?" she asked, then added for emphasis, "I'd like it if you could, if you can."

"Yes, let's do it. I'm excited to see what you've got."

Gina finished the last bite of her food, the last swallow of her drink. "I'll pay, since officially you're the client."

Kenzo looked a little disconcerted by that comment. Gina wondered if he was insulted by the "client" remark, maybe he was thinking he was more of a friend? Next time she would let him pay.

After she paid, they left the izakaya and once outside Kenzo said that he didn't recognize the two men. "But I'm not certain I could say I've never seen them before, nor that they hadn't been at the poetry club or the Bar. They just didn't look familiar."

"I know what you mean," said Gina. "I'm not sure either."

Kenzo glanced back over his shoulder after they walked for a few steps. "I don't see them following us anyway."

"It's probably just my imagination," Gina said.

Gina and Kenzo sipped beers while she set up her laptop and extra monitor. She briefed him on the program—the underlying functions, the data structures, and the remaining modules to complete. He made some polite comments, and some smart comments.

After bringing fresh, cold beers from the fridge, Gina launched the simple web interface to the demo AKIKAZE.

"It doesn't look like much right now. I'm not much of an interface designer."

"Don't worry about that," he said with a beery grin. "It's a demo, a prototype, right?"

"Right," she replied. "Okay, here we go."

She showed him how to select a set of poems stored in the database by entering in a search term. "Say for example, 'mushroom.'"

Kenzo typed in the word. In less than a breath, a list of poem titles or first few words appeared on the screen.

Gina pointed to the screen, their shoulders touching lightly. "You can click a title, or first few words, to see the entire poem. Or you can click the checkbox to select a poem to be added to a list of those poems to be used in the story creation. When you are satisfied with your selections, you click the 'create' button to write the story."

She demonstrated by clicking on a poem starting "A petal of sunlight." The expanded poem came up:

> A petal of sunlight
> rests on a mushroom
> before dying.

She opened a couple of other poems, gave him time to read them, then clicked the button. After several moments, the program responded with a few lines of text:

> In a wooded glen, a mushroom grows on an ancient tree. It waits for sunlight, which is needed for it to grow. When some light falls on it, the mushroom soaks it up and is joyful, even as the ray of light no longer lives.

Kenzo said, "Nice."

Gina wasn't sure if he meant the poems and mini-story, or how they came up on the screen. "The story is a bit dry," she said. "But it's a start."

He studied the screen for a few moments, then started to play with the program while sipping beer. Gina fixed them some snacks, and kept their beers from being empty for too long.

After a couple more beers, Kenzo sat back. "It's cool. Fun. Kind of like your news summary app, but starting with poetry and creating a story. It's more interesting. And more difficult to program, I would imagine."

Gina said, "Thanks! Is it something with enough promise to continue working on?"

"I think so."

Disappointed with the weak response, she said, "Okay. Let me know how I could modify it so that it's something the Society could use."

"How about Yurika's poetry group?"

"She didn't seem interested. Do you think we could show her the demo, so I could get her feedback?"

"I'll ask."

"Thanks."

They sat quietly for a moment, before Gina asked, "Would you like to stay the night?"

Kenzo smiled his shy smile.

They didn't sleep much, and Kenzo left early to stop at home before going to work. Gina sipped a cup of coffee and cleaned up the kitchen while the sheets were washing. The demo went well with Kenzo, she thought. The sex was good too, more relaxed, even playful. Maybe it was all the poetry. Or beer.

When the sheets were finished in the washer, she put them in the dryer, took a shower, then headed for work. She was getting into work as the others were settling in. So, good that she wasn't too late.

She met with her team, and they finalized the list of potential clients and possible applications: a recycling company (automated sorting), a medical diagnostic machine manufacturer (embedded hardware and software for AI), and a graphics font designer (font recognition and automated design).

Tokunaga made a low sigh.

Gina said to him, "What is it?"

"These are all good projects and companies. But how do we sell them with our limited experience in these areas?"

"Good point," said Morita.

"Let's divide and conquer. We each take one, find out more about the company, then write up a story about how we can help them. We don't focus on our lack of experience."

Tokunaga and Morita glanced at each other.

"What is it?" Gina asked.

Morita said, "We were talking about marketing by telling a story, and we don't think that we, the two of us, are good at it. We feel that it's difficult to do without making the story seem not serious enough."

Tokunaga said, "Maybe we are just techies without much creativity, but we'd feel more comfortable with just a standard presentation."

Gina felt a wave a frustration, but then came a cancelling wave of empathy for them. She sensed their morale was low. "Okay, I understand. Let's take one company each, research them, and come up with ideas for a presentation. Don't worry about the story part for now."

They nodded, but without much enthusiasm.

As the meeting was breaking up, Gina asked Morita if he'd been able to expand the data storage.

"Yes, didn't you get the notification?"

"No." That's strange, she thought.

"That's strange," echoed Morita as if reading her mind. "Maybe Yamashita-san's ghost has been at it again."

Gina laughed. "Maybeee."

Beep, beep, beep

Gina woke up, glared at the clock. It wasn't the culprit.

Then she remembered she'd inserted a couple lines of code in AKIKAZE to alert her when the port error occurred. She rolled off her futon and stretched like a cat before checking out the commotion. Her laptop had fired up, AKIKAZE was running, and the alert message blared in a popup:

Error 630: port open

Gina turned off the alarm, opened the log, and found that the port was indeed open. She clicked to open the program's dialogue box and typed in a quick line.

Hello. Who are you?

Gina watched the throbber show the program was working. When the animated spinning stopped, this appeared in the dialogue box:

Hello world! Not really a 'you' here.

What the fuck! Then another line of dialogue appeared:

Think point of view.

"What?"

What?

The throbber wheel spun for a second or two.

Omniscient Narrator.

Gina squeezed into a packed train car heading to the Society to meet Kenzo. She'd spent about half of the work day researching her potential client —the graphics and font designer. The company and its products seemed the most esoteric of the three potential clients, so she volunteered for it. The first part of a potential application or demo project—the font recognition—was likely to be straightforward. It would be a machine-learning classification task, feeding the algorithm thousands of labeled examples. This is Helvetica. Not Helvetica. Helvetica. Not Helvetica ...

The second part—automated font creation—would be difficult. No, that's understated. It would be a fucking pain. Gina found a few online examples of font design programs, but they were designed for amateur consumers not professionals. Real font designers take months, as long as a year, to create a full font set. The number of parameters and subjective decisions would be tremendous, not to mention running a search to ensure the generated fonts don't tread too closely to an already trademarked font. But that's what would make an automated font design application so compelling—reducing the time and cost involved.

Of course the designers would be skeptical that the creative process could be automated. Not to mention that they would not want to be programmed out of a job. Her presentation, the story, that she and the team come up with would need to address both of those issues.

The other team members were still working on their research when she left, sneaking out actually. She wanted show Kenzo progress she made on AKIKAZE. She was also hoping to get more data from him.

The train arrived at the stop and she climbed the stairs to the street. She glided into the stream of pedestrians going her way. As she neared the Society, she started looking around, reflexively, for anyone looking especially nondescript. Most people are "descript," she decided.

When she got to the Society, the receptionist was leaving for lunch.

"You can wait here for Karaki-san," he said.

"Thank you. How did your holo-monitor work today?"

The question appeared to fluster him. "What? Oh, the computer? It was mostly fine. It only froze about ten times today. So far."

"That's not good. I'd be happy to look at it. I owe Kenzo a favor or two anyway."

"Cool," he said, pulling his bag onto his shoulder. "Go for it." With that he flew out the door.

Gina sat at the desk, tried to see where the projector was located. She hadn't gotten very far, when Kenzo appeared through the wall, or rather the fake wall.

"I hope you're better than our last receptionist," he said.

Gina laughed. "Actually, I might need a new job."

"Oh?"

"Just kidding," she said. "I was talking with the receptionist before he left. He was telling me again about the glitches with the holographic system. I told him I'd be willing to see if I could find what's wrong."

Kenzo said, "That would be great. The technician for the company is getting tired of coming over here."

"All right, I'll see if I can do that soon. No promises. Anyway, I'm intrigued by the system."

"Sounds good. Tea or coffee? Hot or iced?"

"Iced coffee sounds great."

He went through the wall to the refreshment center, and returned with cans of cold coffee. They went back to his office and sipped the drink while Gina set up her laptop. She connected to Society WiFi and pulled up the program. She told him she added a couple of features and tweaked some of the algorithms. "Nothing major, mainly backend improvements. I hope they improve the experience for the members of the poetry club."

When it was running, Kenzo tried it out. "I see," he said. "It's definitely more responsive. And the story results are more, um, nuanced? If that's the right word."

"That's a good word," Gina said. "I'll take that. I've added a rule generating algorithm that might be helping. There is one thing that would help further."

Kenzo looked up from the screen. "More data?"

Gina laughed. "Of course. Always more data. The program even asks for it."

Kenzo looked puzzled.

Gina added, "Well, in a non-literal, programmatic way."

Kenzo nodded slowly. "Wow, that's cool. What kind of data and how much?"

"Another set the same size would be helpful, similar kinds of poems or time frame, if that's possible. It helps with validation of the algorithms."

"I'll see what we can offer," he said, but not too optimistically. "Oh, I talked with Yurika Hamada. She's still skeptical, might even be somewhat antagonistic. Sorry to say."

Gina wanted to sigh in frustration. "What do you think we can say to alleviate her concerns?" Then she added, "You know, I'm not clear on what they do."

"I'm afraid I haven't been able to explain it well."

"No, it's not your fault," she said.

"But, she didn't say no, either."

"I guess that is a little encouraging."

"You might have better luck than me."

"Okay, thanks. I'll follow up with her."

"To tell you the truth," he said under his breath. "I think they are involved in something deeper than a poetry club."

"Something deeper?"

He shrugged. "I don't know. Just a feeling."

Gina didn't press him. "By the way, can you take a few hours off work? Maybe tomorrow morning?"

"I should be able to. Why?"

"Have you ever wanted to play detective?"

The train stopped at the station nearest to her mother's house. Gina and Kenzo got off and went to the nearest hotel and checked in.

"All right," Kenzo said when he opened the door to their room. There was a round bed, glitter lights, mirrors all around, a bowl of condoms on the dresser. He dropped onto the bed.

They enjoyed the room, woke up early, and enjoyed it again.

"We better get going," Gina said as she went to the shower.

They got dressed and walked the short distance to her mother's house. At a coffeeshop near the house, they got a table and ordered coffee and pastries.

Gina gulped her coffee. "Ok, I'll head over and let her know I'm here. If she keeps to her pattern, she'll leave about mid-morning. I'll come out just behind her to make sure you see her. Then all you have to do is follow her. She's usually gone for at least two hours, so when you find out where she's been you can come back here. I'll be waiting. Good?"

"Yep."

Gina went over to the house, and looked back to Kenzo before she went in. He gave her a thumbs-up. She smiled at his goofy expression.

Inside the house, Gina called out, "Hello, Mom."

There was no response, but there were the sounds of the television on low volume. The entryway was as untidy as it had been, maybe even a little worse. She slipped off her shoes and stepped into the house. She found her mother eating a rice ball at the low table with a book open. A travel show was on the TV—it looked like a hill town in Tuscany.

"How are you?" Gina asked.

Kumi swallowed and said, "Gina."

Um, yes? "Yep," Gina said.

Kumi seemed satisfied with that answer, and she raised her nearly finished rice ball.

Gina assumed she was being offered a rice ball. "No thanks. I just ate."

Kumi went back to her book and TV show and rice ball. Gina opened her laptop and feigned working.

"What are you doing?" her mother asked.

Gina almost jumped up at the question. "Remember I told you about the story creation from poetry? You told me about aesthetic rules being evident from sexual attraction?"

Kumi munched on the last bite of rice ball. "Huh?"

"The aesthetic rules ..." Gina sighed then skipped over the repetition. "I'm adding rules, although AKI—the program needs more data too. Can you help me?"

Kumi went over to a stack of file folders, picked out a few and handed them to Gina.

"I'll be back later," her mother said.

"Okay," Gina said. "Have fun."

Kumi gave Gina a squint, maybe wondering what that meant.

When she was out the door, Gina hurried to the entryway. She peeked out—Kumi was heading the direction she had the other day. Gina looked over to the coffeeshop. Kenzo was already walking after her mother. He gave Gina a quick wave as he fell in step with Kumi.

While her mother was gone, Gina looked through the files, some were receipts, a collection of old research papers, and more of the squares of paper with strange notes and pseudocode written on them. Then she found several pages of printouts of coded programmatic functions. Not sure she could take the pages, she snapped photos.

Wondering what else her mother had in the files, Gina looked through them, but there was nothing related to programming. But she did find a stack of poetry books, mostly erotica. She lined them up and snapped photos of their covers.

Not long after she'd finished, Kenzo opened the door to the house. "I'm back."

Gina went to the entryway. "Did you—?"

Kenzo, wide-eyed, said, "Wow."

On the train later that afternoon, Gina said, "Wow."

Kenzo nodded.

Before they left for the train station, he'd shown her the smallish book and art store in the warren of shops. Crammed in the store were rows of bookshelves, all the titles in the genre of erotic sensuality. On the walls were prints in the same genre. The owner of the shop, around sixty, with a neatly trimmed salt-and-pepper beard, welcomed them nonchalantly, as if he were selling greeting cards and stationary.

She and Kenzo looked around for a while, Gina admittedly feeling the effects of the eroticism, though it was entwined with the wonder of what her mother was doing in the shop. She asked Kenzo if he could see what her mother was up to. He said he only passed by a couple of times, not wanting to arouse suspicion. All he noticed was Kumi looking at the books.

Before they left the store, Gina picked out a book of erotic poetry. The owner claimed she'd made a good choice. She almost asked him about her mother, but decided it might be an awkward discussion so she paid for the book and left.

On the train ride home, they were reading the poetry when Kenzo slowly slid his hand up her thigh.

10.1

Lastly, a Few Years Ago

Yurika sipped Yamazaki whiskey while Harumi read the manifesto. Yurika tracked her friend's eye movements, knowing which words were being scanned and hoped they were being knitted into their intended meaning. It was a lengthy treatise, so Harumi took more than a couple of minutes to read it all, including retracing a line or two to three.

But its essence could be summed succinctly: Poetry is and always was for everyone, to provide a voice to the mystery of life, of death, of love, of grief, of loneliness. Ubiquitous in all things and thoughts. No one owns poetry nor is it governed by the self-proclaimed few fortifying their dominions. Rather, poetry is suffocated by power; it exists to empower. It's exemplified by the poetry of the Dark Ravine. Please join us to overthrow the citadels of poetic hegemony.

Harumi looked up, blinked once, twice. "I'd be honored to be the first to join."

11

Into a Deep, Dark Well

Diving deeper into a deep, dark well, the poet, seeking to prove his worth as a priest, found a frayed purification wand in a closet. He could use it to bless the kiln, if he knew where to find it.

Taking a risk that night, Akikaze left the shrine with his journal and a charcoal writing stick. He decided to be more organized in his approach to his life in the village, so he started a map roughly sketched from his memory. Next to each building, he noted the people who lived in it, if it was a home, or noted the building's purpose, if it wasn't. Besides creating the map, he wanted to find the kiln he was supposed to bless, apparently should have already blessed.

Earlier, when he found that the mushroom soup woman, his first poetry student, had vanished after seeing his journal, he thought about running after her to explain. He would make up something. For instance, he wrote his journal as a fantasy in which he imagined himself as a wandering poet.

No, she wouldn't believe a word of it.

Then again, maybe she hadn't actually read his journal. Maybe she jostled the table getting up to leave. That seemed unlikely given her sudden disappearance.

Then if, or when, she confronted him about it, what would he say? That was a good question. Would he blurt out the un-lacquered truth about the real priest? Would he explain his continuing impersonation as evidence of goodwill? Of filling in for the priest until he returned? Of his efforts to find the priest?

But really, those were lame, unbelievable explanations. All he knew was that he didn't want to leave, not

Hi.

> Hi.

The well, in this case, is a metaphor representing the character's current situation. Diving in, metaphorically, the character, the poet, has decided to accept his plight, at least to some degree. He gives into the situation, that is, into the life of the village, and into his role as the substitute priest. The "deep, dark" description implies the well, the village life, is still unknown, and perhaps, dangerous.

> Are wells always dangerous? I suppose, although they provide life-giving water.

Hmm, yes, they provide water. They could also be shallow, that is, not so dangerous. So, it seems the adjectives used are necessary to qualify the metaphor.

Symbolically, $C(t+1) = C(t) + p$ [Where the character's development, $C(t+1)$, is based on the current character, $C(t)$, modified by a phrase, p, in this case a metaphor].

> I can see how that would work.

Hopefully in the story, S, it will as well.

right then.

He continued his work on his map, filing in the details he could, which weren't many—the charcoal maker, the large teahouse-like building, the mother with the two children, and of course, the mushroom soup woman's house.

Not finding a kiln, at least what he thought what a kiln would look like, he widened his search. In the dark, away from the village perimeter, the going was rough, and with only the dullest gray moonlight imaginable he tripped more than once. The night was quiet; only a few crickets voiced their loneliness. He tried to walk as carefully as possible, to avoid tripping, but also not to make noise and alert the village to his presence.

Just as he was about to give up, he found the kiln. Next to it, was a long stack of firewood about waist high. He drew its location on his map, and satisfied, began to retrace his steps, only glancing at the mushroom soup woman's house as he passed it.

Back in the shrine, in the yellow light from the lantern, he worked on a poem about searching for the kiln. The words came without thought, from his gut, viscerally poetic. He wrote until he dropped the brush and let himself sink to his side onto the comforting mat.

The mushroom soup woman arrived at the shrine early in the morning. Akikaze was already awake, trying to repair the purification wand. A five-year-old could have done better.

"Good morning," they said at the same time.

She brought him breakfast, and she set it out for him.

"I can finish fixing that," she said.

Before he could say that she didn't need to, she took it from him. "You need it to bless the kiln," she said. "The sooner the better."

"You heard," Akikaze said.

"Yes. I wasn't eavesdropping, but she was speaking loudly."

Akikaze shook his head. "She was insistent."

The mushroom soup woman worked for a while, then said, "You seem a little quiet today."

"I'm sorry. I must have not slept well."

She nodded. Akikaze was beginning to feel relieved. It didn't seem as if she was going to say anything about the journal.

He said, "I was thinking about the festival, the idea for poetry being interspersed in the lighting ceremonies."

"I was speaking out of turn," she said quickly. "I can't speak for you, or for the village, in what happens at the festival."

"I see, but I was going to say that it's a good idea. I fully support it."

"But we will need to have the rest of the village support it."

"Perhaps, if more of the villagers were involved." Akikaze put down his bowl. "If we could get several to create a verse or two of poetry, we could perform a renga. Do you think you can convince a few to be involved?"

"I don't know," she said. "I'll ask some who might be willing. What do I tell them about renga?"

"It's five-seven-five-seven-seven syllables. One person starts with a verse, then the second plays off of the first, and so on. It's best if there is a theme. How about if it's related to the history of the village?"

She thought for a moment as she creased a piece of the pure white paper on the wand. "I see, that could be a good theme. Although, I don't know very much about the history, so I can't say for sure."

"I understand. Would someone else in the village know more?"

She asked him, "Don't you know about the history?"

Akikaze went cold. He should have anticipated that. "Surprisingly, I don't know very much either."

She thought again. "The village elder must know all the history. You could ask him."

"All right," he said, slowly. Then he added, "It might be good for both of us to talk with him."

"Maybe so," she said. She put the wand on the table. "All finished. Although I just realized I shouldn't have touched it. I'm a woman, after all. We're impure."

"It's all right, I can re-purify it," he said, realizing he'd made another mistake as a priest. Even though he didn't believe she could make anything impure.

As if she could hear his thoughts, her cheeks had reddened to the shade of the season's first plum blossoms.

Alone again, Akikaze read more of the priest's records, and wondered why the simple words struck him as so profound. Perhaps because they were just that—simple. And yet they encapsulated so much life, so much more life than he, Akikaze, had lived.

Of course, he couldn't ask the priest, the real priest, what motivated him to write them in the first place. Nor could he ask why go to the trouble of writing them if he wasn't going to expand on the meaning behind the record. Maybe the answer was in the records. Akikaze opened an earlier book. And there in the first few records was this:

> Blessed the marriage of the mushroom grower and his wife.

After purifying the wand with a sprinkle of salt—he'd seen priests purifying other objects with salt—Akikaze put on the formal robes, hat, toed socks, and wooden sandals. It all fit perfectly. So far, he was doing well in upgrading his priestly image. Although, he did need to be more careful; the mistake he made allowing the mushroom soup woman to touch the purifying wand was a bad one. He couldn't afford to make another error like that.

Now, for the purification ceremony he had to perform. Using the purifying wand would be simple—a few shakes here and there. But there was also the prayer. The priest surely kept a book of chants or some other record of chants. If he could find that, he might be able to pull off his priestly life.

In the cabinet drawer, there were scrolls of chants. It wasn't obvious which would work for the blessing of a kiln. Perhaps it didn't matter, though. A chant was a chant, wasn't it? But he didn't want to just get by. He wanted to excel, as if in competition with his predecessor.

He picked one of the chants. It had a line about water reeds and the gods that inhabited them. There wasn't much to it, a repetition of three lines, then four, then three. He memorized them. He wondered what else he needed to bring. Not at all sure, he brought some incense, some salt, and a cup for water.

Walking carefully in the wooden sandals, he headed to the village, silently practicing the chant. It should be easy, he thought. Wave the wand say the chant. Sprinkle salt and splash water.

It must have been a cloudy day, as the morning light was even less bright than usual. He suddenly missed the sky, a brilliant blue autumn sky. The nostalgia started a wave of poetry fragments in his head. Feeling a wave of confidence, he started to insert and replace words, then whole phrases in the chant with his own.

Before he knew it, he was at the edge of the village. A few villagers were going about their business. A couple walking toward him bowed and stepped aside in deference.

"Good morning," he said.

They looked up in surprise, and repeated his greeting. He hurried past, wondering why they'd be surprised.

He came to the mushroom soup woman's home. Hoping he could restore his viability as a priest, more importantly a poet priest, he deviated from the path and went to her home.

"Good morning," he called out at the doorway.

She came to the door almost immediately. With only a glance at his finery, she invited him in.

"I can't stay," he said.

"Then you're on your way to the kiln blessing then. Not returning from it."

"Yes, I'm going there now. I stopped to invite you along."

"Oh?"

He thought of a quick excuse: "Well, in case she isn't there to observe me, I thought it would be good to have a witness that the ceremony was performed."

She smiled in understanding. "Of course. Let me change. Please come inside."

He considered if he was allowed in her home wearing the priest's robes. He didn't know if it was against protocol, but he'd made enough errors already.

"Thank you, but I should wait outside."

"Yes, of course," she said.

She went back in. Out of the corner of his eye, Akikaze could partially see her taking off her house kimono. He looked away.

She was quickly ready. On the way there, she said, "I again mentioned to the village elder your idea of using the village history in the poetry and the festival. I don't think he understands. Maybe if you explained it to him."

Akikaze's confidence dipped. "I suppose I could try. But I don't want to push something he wouldn't want to do."

"Perhaps if we could give him a better idea of how it might work."

"How would we do that?"

She took a couple of steps before saying, "We could show him how a renga would be performed, just two or three lines. Like you taught me."

"You and I?" he asked, although he wasn't sure that it would be a good idea for him to be so close to the elder.

They arrived at the kiln and the woman was there with her husband and children. They were arranging wood in the hearth.

"Just in time," she said.

They stepped aside to make room for him and the mushroom soup woman.

The kiln woman asked him, "Do you need some water?"

"Yes, please," he said.

While she brought over a wooden bucket of water sitting next to the wood stack, likely in case it caught fire, he set up his wand and salt container on a rock. He dipped the bamboo ladle into the water bucket, and filled the ladle. He offered the water first over the hands of all present, then with a fresh ladle of water, let each take a sip, ending with himself.

Next, he opened the container of salt and, as he had seen before, sprinkled a pinch of salt in front of him as he walked to the kiln. Stopping there, and with a fresh pinch, he sprinkled salt along the front perimeter of the kiln.

He went back to the rock, placed the salt container on it, and took his wand back to the kiln. He glanced at the mushroom soup woman as he held it in front of him like a sword. The sheaves of paper were freshly creased and as white as the salt.

In front of the shrine, he bowed then waved and shook the wand as he intoned his chant, not quite remembering all the words, neither the original nor the ones he'd created on the way.

Speak to us on the strength and endurance of the kiln,
Its power as flexible and tenacious as summer reeds,
Its cry as mournful as autumn winds, weeping.

The family seemed quietly mystified when he finished. Likely it wasn't the same prayer they heard before.

But apparently satisfied, they gave him one of their fired pots. He accepted the gift with a gracious bow. He gathered up his priestly tools, and he and the mushroom soup woman left.

After walking in silence for a few moments, she said, "You've changed."

"I've changed?" Akikaze asked her, his voice barely above a whisper.

"You've changed your ceremonies. The chants and prayers are different," she clarified.

Ah. "I suppose I have changed them. Is that acceptable?"

"It's all for the better." After a pause, she added, "But perhaps you've changed too."

"Because I've changed the prayers?" Akikaze hoped.

"I don't know what I meant. Would you like to come into my home for some food?"

"Thank you, I should go back to the shrine. Take care of the wand and robe."

"Shall I bring something by later?"

"I'd like that. Very much."

The mushroom soup woman arrived with food as promised, and with the elder. He wore a grim, tired look on his face, as if put out he was being dragged to the shrine to consider a change in the village festival that likely had remained unchanged for generations. She, on the other hand, seemed brighter, more cheerful, than he last saw her.

The elder, his hair white and thin on top, long in back and tied in a loose knot, spoke immediately, "I hear you've devised a plan for adding poetry to the autumn festival."

Akikaze looked at the woman then to the elder. What would the priest be saying now? The elder didn't appear to have much respect for the priest, given the tone of his statement.

"Yes, we've discussed it further," Akikaze said.

The woman said, "We've been learning poetry, the priest has surprised us with his knowledge of poetry and his wonderful ability to write poems."

The elder gazed at the poet priest, saying nothing. Akikaze shrank within the shadows of the shrine.

Akikaze said, "I appreciate the kindness, but I'm a humbly modest writer of the occasional poem. But she," he almost called her the mushroom soup woman, "has great talent. We should use that ability and others in the village to add to the festival. Her wonderful idea was to write a renga centered around the history of the village."

He waited to see if the elder was familiar with renga. The elder didn't raise a question.

Akikaze continued, "We were thinking of having one line of the renga delivered between each of the rounds of the lighting ceremony." He hoped he said that correctly.

The woman took over. "Since I know very little about the history, I couldn't fill in the gaps of what either of us knows. That's why we thought to ask you, since you would be the most knowledgable one in the village."

Akikaze could see his chest swell a little, even in the darkness of the shrine.

"Yes, that's true. I would be the one to ask."

The woman smiled generously. Akikaze nodded deferentially.

The elder cleared his throat. Then he began.

The elder's story was long, with many details. In the short version that Akikaze recreated in his mind, the village had been there for more than a hundred and fifty years. Before the village existed, the ancestors of the current residents lived far away. One of those ancestors became embroiled in a dispute with a court official and a member of the Emperor's retinue during an outbreak of disease and famine.

The dispute escalated and the ancestor was going to be arrested and condemned. He and his family and several supporters and their families escaped one night with nothing more than what they were wearing. In the dark, without a moon, traveling as far as they could in the dark before hiding in a forest during the day. They traveled like that for several days, sipping water from streams, finding wild plants to eat, until they could travel no longer and stopped in the dark ravine. Even after other generations had come and gone, they stayed there, feeling safe only in the darkness.

After recounting the history, the elder asked Akikaze if that would be enough for the poetry part of the festival.

"It's a lot to take in," Akikaze said, looking at the woman. She was sitting quietly. "But I believe so. We will talk about it more, and see if we can come up with a suitable plan."

As the elder got up, the woman said she was going to stay and help clean the shrine. The elder gazed at her, then at Akikaze. Has he finally realized I'm not the priest? Akikaze wondered.

But the elder left without a word.

The mushroom soup woman said, "I only knew that there was some reason for the villager founders escaping from where they came from."

"It's a powerful story," Akikaze said.

"I would like to try write a poem," she said.

She sat down as Akikaze brought over writing materials. He sat down to write his own, working up to something that might work for the festival's renga event. But he could only watch her, poised with brush dipped in ink.

Instead of a poem about the village history, Akikaze wrote this:

Sitting in shadows,
quietly composing,
thinking of her.

As if she heard his poem, she looked up from the paper. With her gaze upon him, she put down the brush. The fingers of both her hands trailed along the edges of her kimono, opening it.

12

A Tiny, Oddly-Shaped Room

"Welcome back," Yurika said when she came over to greet Gina and Kenzo at the poetry club's bar, where they were drinking a smooth, warm sake. A few other members were also in the space, drinking and talking.

"Thank you for inviting us," said Gina.

"Yes, thank you," said Kenzo.

Yurika said, "Enjoy your drinks," and then to Gina, "Actually, I'm glad you contacted me again. I've been thinking about your project. I hope you weren't offended by my statement about it being dangerous. "

"No, not at all," Gina said. "In the technology world, being dangerous is a compliment."

"In what way?"

"A better word might be 'disruptive.' Which implies dangerous, at least to the established companies, or in the established way of thinking."

Yurika nodded. "It's much the same in poetry. I do want to discuss it some more, later this evening. For now, enjoy your drinks. And since you are here, would you like to take part in our warm-up renga?"

Gina and Kenzo looked at each other, waiting for the other to say something. Kenzo said, "Well, I'm not much of a poet, despite looking at poetry databases all day long."

"I'm not a poet at all," Gina said. "Of course, I appreciate good poetry."

Yurika waved away their excuses. "We're all poets. And it's a little fun that we have. Nothing to take too seriously. Well, most of us anyway. Please accept."

Gina looked at Kenzo, "I will if you will."

Kenzo grimaced, then shrugged and said "Okay,

sure. Let's do it."

Yurika said, "Excellent! Enjoy."

The groups formed at the tables, Kenzo and Gina sitting apart. Gina's group consisted of three others. One of them explained the simple rules, first checking that Gina knew the numbers of syllables for each line.

"Five-seven-five-seven-seven," said the others at the same time. The teams would choose the order of each person's contribution. Then the topic would be announced. The first person would create their line, then read it. The next person would add to the poem in the allotted time.

The renga started with the general topic of summer heat. At Gina's table, the other woman was first up. Her name was Harumi. Her midnight blue hair poked out from under a black beret. A good look for her. With only two minutes to produce her first line, Gina wondered what Harumi was thinking, what her poetic processes involved. Gina made some notes waiting for her turn—second from last, a seven-syllable line: heat, sweat, running AC, finding shade. Nothing too exciting, maybe too obvious.

After what seemed like a minute, the bell rang. Harumi sighed and read her line:

Crow's cry burns away.

The second stanza came after the next bell from a middle-aged man named Yusuke. It was about a young boy and girl waiting in the heat for a train.

Hmm, thought Gina, not sure where this was going. It wouldn't do much good to write something ahead of her turn, she decided, if the lines were going to be less than obvious.

The third line evoked a tsunami of sunlight washing over the city. The clock started for her turn. She wished for two, or three, times her two minutes. With only a few seconds left, she wrote:

Nondescript men drinking beer.

The bell rang. She finished the last word and looked up. Her teammates were looking back expectantly. She smiled, shrugged, and read her line.

Her teammates looked confused at first, then one laughed, then another. When one applauded, the others followed suit. Gina laughed and applauded her team.

After the renga game, there was a break before the next part of the meeting. Yurika asked Gina to follow her. Gina glanced at Kenzo, who was talking with a couple of the poets.

"Did you enjoy the renga?" asked Yurika when they were in a tiny, oddly-shaped room. The space had two angled corners and two round corners. The door was off-centered on one wall. The four chairs and a table weren't centered in the room. There was a bookcase with glass doors that looked like a tansu cabinet, normally seen under a set of stairs, its pattern following the steps upward.

"I did in the end," said Gina. "I didn't think I could be of much help for our team."

"It sounded like you did more than help."

"They were just being polite."

Yurika laughed. "I can't recall us ever being polite about anything."

Gina demurred with a smile. "Notwithstanding that, thank you for letting me and Kenzo participate."

"You're welcome. How is your AI program coming along?"

"Thanks for asking. It's a process of success and failure." Gina reminded herself to tell a story. She repeated the one she told Kenzo, about waking up wondering how 'raincloud' was used in a set of poems, running a search on the terms, and then getting not only the results but how the resonance of the poems created a story.

"I'd like to show you the prototype, rather than explain it further. If you're still interested in seeing it, when you have time, perhaps, later this evening? We'd need to go somewhere we can connect to my server. Perhaps at the Society?"

Yurika said, "Admittedly, I'm both skeptical and intrigued. So, yes, I'd like to see your prototype."

"Excellent," Gina said.

"If I may, I'd like to bring two other members of the Project."

"Of course."

"However," Yurika said, raising a hand as if to stop traffic, "If I find your program too supportive of the established powers in poetry, I would

Hey there.

> Hey.

An oddly-shaped room ... make that a tiny, oddly-shaped room, provides a setting detail. The room's unusualness in size and shape impart a sinister feel to the reader. "Tiny" would induce claustrophobia in those so affected, likely to some degree in most readers.

"Oddly-shaped" will raise readers' interest. Why is the room oddly-shaped? Or more specifically, does the room have a reason for being shaped irregularly?

Symbolically, $d(1) + d(2) + ... d(n) \rightarrow R(i)$ [Where the sum of setting details, d, influence reader engagement or intensity, $R(i)$].

> There might be a limit in the number of details, too many might be lost on the reader.

That's good feedback. One telling detail might be worth many. The story, S, could dictate which to include.

ask you to destroy it."

Gina wasn't sure she heard that right. When it sunk in that it was what Yurika said, Gina didn't know what to say in response. She'd never been confronted so directly about her work. It's just a program, she wanted to say. It's designed to help you, others, with research. But in her head that sounded weak, and instead, she gave Yurika a nod. "All right, I'll agree to that."

"All ready," Kenzo said. He'd set up a virtual screen and connection to a computer in the media room at the Society. All the staff had left for the day. They were waiting for Yurika to join them.

"I have a question," Gina said while they set up a tea service.

"Yes?"

"Yurika wants me to destroy the program if it doesn't fit with her agenda. Do you think she was serious?"

Kenzo said, "That seems severe. I don't know her well enough to say if she was serious. Maybe just dramatic?"

"It seemed more than that," Gina said. "She seemed very serious."

"They're here."

On the monitor Kenzo pointed to, Gina saw that Yurika and two others were waiting at front of the Society. Both of the others had been on her renga team—Harumi, the stylish literature professor, and Yusuke, who was a specialist in Shinto poetry.

Kenzo and Gina let them inside and escorted them to the media room.

Gina said, "Thank you for coming. I know it's getting late. And thank Karaki-san for allowing us to meet here. Please help yourself to the tea or coffee."

The three poetry club members acknowledged that with a little bow of their heads. After they got cups of tea, Gina began her presentation, starting with the short version of the story-creating program, briefly noting the resonance of poetry she experienced and how she was curious if that could be captured in a program. This led her to the Society, meeting Kenzo, and how the database provided the poems the program used. She brought up the literary rules, but didn't dwell on that. She briefly told the story of how she found the poet Akikaze and recounted the raincloud story, mentioning she'd already told it to Yurika.

She paused there. The three guests had blank expressions. Assuming that meant they had no questions, or were waiting for the demo to begin, she showed them the interface and steps as she had with Kenzo. The program responded a little differently, as she'd updated some functions.

But it worked well, at least it seemed so to Gina. Kenzo gave her a slight uptick of his eyebrows in support when she glanced at him.

Yurika did not raise her eyebrows, in support or otherwise. After a moment she said, "Interesting concept. I can't say that I understand much of the program, but of course, the bottomline is the question of value. That is, does it provide something of value for what we do as a group."

Gina said, "Absolutely. I can answer any questions, if that would help determine the value."

Yurika glanced at the other two. They were sitting back in their chairs with arms crossed, but didn't ask any questions.

Yurika said to Gina, "Would it be possible for us to have a few minutes alone to try your program and discuss it?"

Gina looked at Kenzo. "If it's okay with Kenzo, it's okay with me."

He nodded. "Yes, it's fine. We can wait in my office."

"Thank you," said Yurika.

Gina said as they were leaving, "Help yourself to more tea."

Yurika gave her a gracious smile.

In Kenzo's office, he said, "What do you think?"

"I suppose it could have been worse. They didn't get up and leave. Or laugh at it."

"I suppose. I wonder what they're doing with the program."

"Can we ...? No, never, mind."

Kenzo gave her a wry smile. "The room is part of our internal video system, but ..."

"No, we shouldn't." After a pause she said, "I could monitor what they are doing on the system. Of course, it's logging their actions anyway so I can always check."

They sat in silence for a while.

Gina said, "I could use some of that tea."

"I can get us some from the lobby station."

"Great," she said. "I'll go with you."

When they got their tea, Gina said, "I could use some fresh air too."

"Good idea," said Kenzo. He opened the front door, and the two went outside.

Gina noticed two men moving away from the building.

"I think that's them," Gina said.

Kenzo looked in the direction she was pointing. "Where?"

"There ..." But they'd disappeared in the dark.

The next morning, Gina arrived at ReMoTe before anyone else. She fixed a cup of scalding hot, strong coffee, and logged into her computer.

She'd managed only a couple of hours of sleep after the meeting with Yurika and the other poetry club members. When they emerged from the media room at the Society, Yurika said they needed to discuss it further. Gina's stomach curled into a ball, feeling that meant "No" and they just didn't want to drop it on her in person. But Gina politely thanked them for their time as well as the enjoyable evening at the poetry club's meeting.

When they left, Kenzo said he didn't know what Yurika meant, other than she might have meant what she said. On the other hand, Gina thought, Yurika didn't seem like a person to have a problem with being direct. Maybe there was still a chance.

After they left, Gina checked the logs and found they had been on the system for less than five minutes. They had entered the search term "dark ravine." AKIKAZE dutifully created:

> Between the mountains, a small valley receives little sunlight. The ever present shadows permeate the lives of those who live there.

"They must not have been impressed. That's all they tried."

"Your presentation must have been good," Kenzo said, obviously trying to spin it positively. "They didn't need to see any more to impress them."

"Thanks," Gina said, "but I don't know about that."

They called it a night after that, going their separate ways, both claiming to need sleep before going to work. Gina felt a little sad going home alone. Perhaps Kenzo was too?

Before finishing a second cup of coffee, she blasted through creating a presentation for the graphics and typeface design company. She relied on her story format—a new client approaches the company for a typeface for all communications, they would like it done in a month, not the usual six months to a year. With ReMoTe AI-enhanced font recognition and design, the month would be no problem. She knew it was a bit of a dream at this point, but it should interest them enough to ask for a demo.

The other team members arrived. Tokunaga and Morita said, "Good morning."

Gina asked how their pitch presentations were going.

Morita said, "We worked together until late last night."

Tokunaga yawned. "Very late."

"I need to give Two-san an update this morning. Should I tell him we are ready to go to the companies?"

Morita said, "I think our presentations are ready for you to review."

"Great!" said Gina. "Mine is too. Let's go into a project room."

When they had finished trialing their individual presentations, Gina summoned as much positive feedback as she could come up with. "Nice work. It's obvious we have our own styles, but that's good. There might be a few technical details to massage before we trial them with Two-san."

That seemed to appease them. Gina said she would send them her technical comments within the hour. Then she would schedule a meeting with Two-san. They all agreed to that.

"One other thing," Gina said. "I'm still working on the Poetry Society's demo, getting closer to a project. I was hoping to get more data from them, soon, and was wondering if I could push the data directly from their server to ours."

Morita said, "How much data?"

"I don't know yet," she answered. "I know I mentioned twice as much, but I hope for up to four or five times."

"It's possible to direct transfer with an open port, of course. Just let me know if it's approved and I'll get you the details."

"Thanks," said Gina. "Also, have either of you worked with holographic display monitors?"

She described the one at the Society, explaining that being able to fix it would give them more leverage to become a client.

Tokunaga said, "I've seen them at trade shows, so I know basically how they work. They're similar to any monitor, meaning there's a driver and a card and a projector. It sounds like the problem might be in the sensitivity settings. Just give me a call the next time you're there and have the dashboard open."

"I'll do that," Gina said, hoping it was going to be as easy as that.

After Gina commented on Tokunaga's and Morita's presentations, she met with Two-san and arranged for a review the following morning. She also received his approval for more data space, telling him it was necessary for the demonstration projects for the company pitches, which wasn't a complete falsehood.

That done, she settled in to work on AKIKAZE, which again complained it needed more data, more poems, as if it were starving. Then it opened a window with a new story it had created about a small village's festival.

Interesting, Gina thought, wondering how AKIKAZE came up with the story from the poems. She checked the log and found the poems used in the story, the trace of the algorithm's path through the rules and the neural nets.

There was room for improvement, but Gina smiled at how well it went. It might be the equivalent of an elementary student's attempt at writing a story. It could use more data, as it requested, and the generated rules needed refining. She thought of Kenzo for the first, perhaps her mother for the second.

Telling Tokunaga and Morita she was going to do some more research for her presentation, Gina put her laptop in her bag. "If you have any questions, text me," she said. "Oh, and Morita-san, I may be calling about that holo-monitor later."

He gave her a thumbs up before she hurried away.

13

Darkness Wrapped the Poet

The darkness wrapped the poet, suffocating him with heavy words; could he twist them into a poem and escape to breathe again?

The poet couldn't be dragged from the deepest shadows of the shrine, huddled in a corner, covered with a blanket. Alone, he didn't know what time of night it was, or even if it was night. He woke from the deepest sleep he remembered. He wondered if his intimacy with the mushroom soup woman was a dream, but he knew that was the furthest thing from what really happened.

He curled up and rolled over, feeling the mats for her until he reached the wall. But she was gone, and that was true as well. He pulled the blanket around him, unneeded as the darkness was fully surrounding him. It all should have been the right ingredients for a poem, or several. But there was nothing coming forth.

All he wanted was to be with the woman.

Maybe that *was* the poem.

She did arrive later, after he pulled himself off the mats, cleaned himself and the room. He spent the rest of the time before she arrived cleaning the shrine, at least getting a start on it.

She announced her arrival by clanging the bell and clapping her hands in prayer.

"Good morning," she said when she found him. "Did you sleep well?"

Merely asking that question had a deep meaning to it. Another poem? The thought, the idea, enlivened him.

"I slept well, thank you," he said. "And how well did you sleep?"

Good afternoon (server time).

Good afternoon.

"Darkness wrapped the poet" ... the evocative image furthers the character's embrace of the once dreadful, dangerous darkness. (Alliteration!) Furthering the image to the point of sensuality, the phrase provides a reverberation back to the character's embrace, literally, with the other character—the so-called mushroom soup woman.

That darkness could wrap a person infers this phrase is a figure of speech, closely to anthropomorphizing, that is, giving the darkness human qualities. But at this stage of the story, the darkness has become a character, as much as the autumn wind.

Interesting literary construct, and likely to be controversial to some.

OK/okay, good to know. Symbolically, $o(t\text{-}1) + o(t\text{-}2) + \ldots o(t\text{-}n) =>$ $C(t)$ [Where an inanimate object or element of imagery, o, which has been mentioned or used a number, n, of times, becomes a character at the current time, t].

Yes, it makes sense.

Good!

"Also well. Shall we eat before I help you finish cleaning?" she asked gazing around the shrine. "You've made a very good start."

That made him smile, as if what she'd said had another meaning, again a level of intimacy he was aware of only now, but which had perhaps always been there, and only now coming to light.

"Let's eat," she said.

He hadn't realized how hungry he was, and how little he'd thought about food beyond mere sustenance. Especially when traveling, it was lower in importance, compared with shelter and a bed of some sort for the evening.

As they ate, she said to him, "The elder was suitably in agreement with poetry at the festival."

"Was he?" Akikaze asked.

She nodded. "We, well, you, only have a few days to prepare."

Put that way, Akikaze felt a sudden grip of anxiety. Not only must he be able to perform his duties at the festival, but he must prepare a renga theme.

"What do we do now?" she asked.

He briefly told her what was involved. There should be at least five participants. That means four more, starting with the woman as one.

"Won't you be one of the participants?" she asked.

Not wanting to be on display, he said, "The renga should be performed by the villagers."

She looked confused. "But you're a resident. And the best poet."

He'd never heard those words before. "I'll be happy to help you and them get started."

She cleaned up their meal, then started polishing the railing in front of the altar, careful not to intrude on the altar itself. She said, "I'll need to see who would be willing to join in." She frowned. "But what should I say to convince them? I mean, they'll likely be reluctant to start something new, then present in front of the rest of the village. Do you know what I mean?"

"Yes, I understand," said Akikaze. It was a valid concern. But how to answer? He thought back to what got the woman interested in the first place. And that's all he needed to say.

"I think you can tell them why you enjoy writing poetry."

She brightened. "I'll do that now, if that's fine with you. I can finish cleaning later?"

"No need. I can finish. Good luck."

"Say a prayer for me," she said.

She returned near nightfall, dejected. "I only found three more willing to be part of the poetry group."

Akikaze had planned for that. "One person could read twice."

"Is that allowed?"

"I don't think there are any particular rules that say it's never allowed. It's just not the usual practice."

"If you would agree, you could be the fifth? It would mean so much to the village. And to me."

How could he deny that? Even as he knew it was not a good idea. "Yes, all right. I'll participate."

She bowed low. Then out of the folds of her kimono she removed a jar. "Sake," she said. "In case I needed to convince you."

"I suppose we should drink it anyway," Akikaze said.

"Of course," said the mushroom soup woman.

The late autumn wind picked up, swirling down into the dark ravine. The poetry group was seated in a circle near the cedar in the darkest corner of the grounds of the shrine. The group's poetry sessions had gone well over the past days, at least Akikaze thought so. Beginning with almost no experience at all, like infants, the five students made errors that would have caused an uproar with his teachers and fellow poets, but somehow, they worked them out amongst themselves, or thought they worked regardless of what he pointed out. Over those days, he came to throw out all he had learned, all he would have espoused as correct and poetically strong.

The mushroom soup woman was the best poet, not only because she had a good ear for the rhythm of words joined together, but she was fearless with their extension into a world unfamiliar to Akikaze. A critical poet might say her poems were simple, stripped bare of artifice. She was not writing to impress a fellow poet, or anyone for that matter. What she wrote touched something, somewhere, that not even he knew what her poems reached.

Despite their overall progress, the exercise was not going well. Akikaze had started off with a verse about the cedar tree. To say their poetry was too wooden would be a good pun, but it was worse than that. It became clear no one cared about a poem of the tree.

"After all, it's just a tree," said one.

"Neither the tallest, straightest, or widest," said another.

The mushroom soup woman said, "Maybe that is the poem. Or the essence of the poem. Its ordinariness."

Akikaze understood. It was the same feeling he got when reading the simple entries in the priest's records. It was what the woman had said before, thinking of things in terms of a poem changed how she thought of them, how it changed her idea of herself. But he didn't want to insert himself in the discussion.

One member of the poetry group asked her, "That the tree has little meaning is worthy of a poem?"

The mushroom woman thought for a moment. "Not worthy of a poem, but that fact, that feeling, is the poem."

The others were silent.

Akikaze resisted smiling. And that would be the last line of the poem of the forgettable tree: "The others were silent."

Instead of pointing that out, he suggested they take a break.

Later, the mushroom soup woman returned with a meal. He thanked her. She thanked him again for leading the poetry group.

"I'm sorry it didn't go well," she said.

"It doesn't always go easily." In fact, he thought, it rarely goes well.

"But we don't have much time before the festival."

"I wouldn't worry," he said. "It will go fine."

"I hope so."

The festival day arrived, bringing a wave of anxiety, and only a thread of hope he'd be able to continue his impersonation in front of the entire village. He dressed in the priest's robes, gathered up his purification wand, a few sheets of chants, salt and water cup, and started his walk to the village.

In the cleared square of forest in front of the teahouse, the villagers had set up a portable shrine, a ring of large torches ready to be lighted. Villagers were going into the community teahouse carrying pots and jars. One couple was carrying a large pot of cooked rice. It was the rice farmers. Akikaze shrank back into the shadows.

At least the farmer didn't have his scythe.

The mushroom soup woman was standing with the elder near the entrance of the building and together they bowed to Akikaze. The woman looked at a table near them on the veranda. As there was nothing on top of it, he assumed it was for him to place his priestly accoutrements.

When Akikaze finished, the woman said she needed to help with the food and left him with the elder.

"She was telling me the poetry group has been working hard," the elder said, with a lilt of skepticism.

"Very diligent," said Akikaze. "I'm sure they are anxious about the renga but they'll do well. Especially for their first time."

The elder gazed at Akikaze, likely judging his veracity. "We will see how it goes, won't we?"

Well, yes, we will, thought Akikaze, unsure of what the elder was getting at.

With only a few stumbles and hesitations, Akikaze got through the beginning of the festival, blessing a small portable shrine, the food, and the villagers themselves.

After the men carried around the shrine with loud cries and shouts, the elder announced the beginning of the main ceremony, the lighting of the torches. The villagers gathered around the circle of torches, some sitting on mats they brought. The elder went into a lengthy speech about the addition of the renga poetry to the festival, both disavowing it and taking credit for it.

When he finished, the first torch was lighted, and the mushroom soup woman, who was selected to go first began to write her line of the renga. Akikaze was surprised at how bright the torch was, or maybe it was so bright because of the darkness of the ravine. While they waited for the woman to finish, the torch light grew in brightness.

The mushroom soup woman finished. Her voice started quietly, then grew in strength.

Chased to a ravine

She glanced at Akikaze as she sat down. He gave her a subtle smile and a slight bow of approval. It was good, setting the rest of the renga well, especially not overwhelming them with something cerebral or obtuse.

The next torch was lighted. He was surprised how much that added to the light of the first. He blinked in the brightness. When he looked up, he saw the faces of the villagers, and they were like different people, visible for the first time.

The next participant read her contribution, which wasn't horrible, although it didn't take the poem too far in a new direction, not in an adventurous way, but that was fine for this group's attempt. The other lamps were lighted, the others read their lines, and he remembered little of them, for he already had formed his contribution, the finale.

As he stood up in the full light of all the torches, brighter than he remembered any daylight at midday, there was a disturbance, voices muttering, then gasps. He looked up from his paper where he had brushed his line about autumn wind weeping and saw two figures, both men dressed in traveling clothes but otherwise devoid of description, entering the ring of light.

"Husband," the mushroom soup woman said in an exhale.

One of the two men gave her a bow. Akikaze realized he'd forgotten that her husband would be returning someday. She hadn't requested a prayer for him in many days.

The woman and her husband approached each other. Stopping apart they gave each other a bow, then spoke a few words, quietly enough that Akikaze couldn't hear, and couldn't tell from their expressions the tenor of their conversation. When he looked back to the villagers, he saw that they were now looking at him. Then to the other man who had arrived. They gazed and turned, back and forth.

Akikaze looked at the other man. Other than haggard from a long journey, the man bore no distinctive features. He could have been a wandering poet.

In a loud burst of voices, the villagers were all speaking at once. The topic was, of course, a dispute about who the other man was, the confusion being that some thought he was the priest, and others pointing to Akikaze dressed in priest's robes, refuting the claim.

Then there was a louder voice, coming from a man stepping out of the crowd. It was the scythe-swinging rice farmer. He approached Akikaze, stopped a couple of steps away. He studied the poet's face. He took another step forward, reached out his hands, and put them on Akikaze's shoulders. After looking closely into Akikaze'e eyes, one after the other, he then turned the poet until his face was fully lighted by the festival torches.

The farmer pointed to Akikaze and announced, "Pervert!"

In a loud, profane explosion of accusations and shouts, most of the villagers seemed swayed that the priest, the man in the robes, was not the priest. The mushroom soup woman stepped into the midst of them. "Wait, how can you be sure?"

Akikaze was grateful, but it was futile. He began to back away, slide into the shadows, away from the festival torchlight. He had no plan, instead was ready to stand his ground, ready to fight, but also ready to run.

The rice farmer began to yell louder, relating in sputtering, spittle-laced, details of the day he chased the pervert away. The mushroom soup woman's husband calmly told how he had found the priest wandering, dazed from a fall, when the husband was making his way back from selling his crop of dried mushrooms.

"What about the priest?" yelled someone. "Which one is real?"

"Maybe both?" said the mushroom soup woman.

Several villagers cried out in disbelief.

Finally, the elder shouted for quiet. "It can't be that both men are the priest. I admit I cannot tell them apart in appearance. Yes, the current priest, the one in the robes, seems different now, especially with our new poetry parts of the festival. I shall ask the man who came here now to tell us who he is."

The priest, apparently still dazed, said, "I'm now remembering I have been here before. I remember being a priest. I must be your priest."

Many of the villagers again cried out in confusion. The rice farmer shouted his "pervert" refrain, gesturing toward the shadows away from the torch light where Akikaze was retreating.

The elder turned to Akikaze. "And do you claim to be the priest?"

Akikaze didn't know what to say. Could the poem now come forth? But the words were heavy, laden with too much meaning, and not enough.

Finally, he whispered. "I cannot say. My life is no longer clear. I might be a traveling poet. I might be a priest who writes poetry."

The elder gazed from him to the priest. "It must be that when you came to the village, to the shrine, you are not the priest we once had. That is clearly this other man, as a man could look like another, but in words, they cannot change so much." He paused and looked at Akikaze. "You must leave our village."

The mushroom soup woman cried out, "No!"

The rice farmer again rang out with his accusation. He was joined by the mushroom soup woman's husband, who finally realized there was more to this wandering poet, or priest, and his wife.

The two allies moved toward Akikaze, clearly to attack him. The woman stepped between them.

Akikaze knew he was doomed unless he ran.

As he turned and ran toward the darkest corner of the dark ravine, he shouted, "I'm not a pervert!"

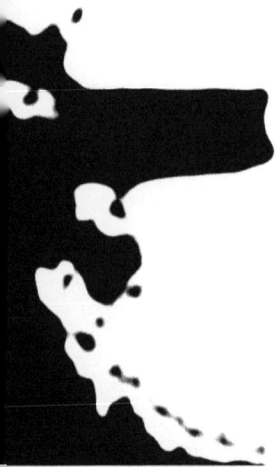

14

A Kernel of Story

Gina arrived at the Society after it was closed to the public. She peered inside the sidewalk-to-cloud windows. The receptionist was not there, probably gone for the day. Kenzo came down to the lobby when she texted him.

He unlocked and opened the door. "Thanks for coming over."

She texted him earlier that she would be able to stop by to see if she could help with the holo screen. "I hope I can help," she said.

"What do I need to do?" he asked.

"Could you power up the receptionist's computer so I can troubleshoot? You don't have to wait around."

"Sure." Kenzo sat down and started the computer. "I have a report to finish. Just text me if you need anything."

"I'll do that."

When he left, she played around with holo monitor, then found the dashboard and tried out a few of the settings to see their effect on the monitor. Satisfied she would be able to test out some adjustments, she searched for the database manager she'd seen Kenzo use.

Finding that, she located the largest dataset of poems. She entered the ReMoTe server address and the port Morita had opened. With a twinge of guilt, she started sending the dataset.

While the upload progressed, she called Tokunaga for his help with the adjustments of the holo monitor. They made a couple of tweaks that seemed to stabilize the screen's positioning, and made the touch interaction

more consistent.

Before they ended the call, Gina asked Tokunaga, "So, how was your afternoon?"

"You mean finishing our presentations?"

Gina laughed. "Yes, how did that go?"

"We finished the changes. Thanks for your comments."

"What do think of them?"

"Well, honestly, I think they are very good."

"Great! Then we should land some new contracts?"

Tokunaga sucked in a little air. "We shall see."

"Good luck to us," Gina said.

"Good luck there too," Tokunaga said.

"Thanks," she said.

When Kenzo came into the lobby, Gina showed him the changes to the holo-monitor.

"Cool, thanks," he said. "I'm sure the receptionist will appreciate this immensely."

"I hope it works for him. If not, he can call me and I might be able to help him make further adjustments."

"I'll let him know."

"Did you finish your report?" Gina asked as she began to shut down the computer.

"Yes. Too many reports to write in this job," he said.

"They're a pain. I suppose it makes managers happy to require them. Justifies their jobs."

Kenzo nodded. "Would you like to go out for a drink, or meal? Or both?"

"I would, of course, but I should go back to working on business presentations. Maybe tomorrow?"

"Tomorrow, for sure. If I don't have another report to write."

Back at the office, Gina checked the uploaded dataset on the server. It had transmitted without errors. It was large, too much to download to her laptop. She would have to take a subset, or just work on it from the office.

She went to get a cup of coffee. Sitting down with the coffee, she opened up AKIKAZE. The program had been running in the background and started consuming the poetry database. As the program crawled through the upload data, she recalled a few lines her mother had written in tiny print. She found it her her photos:

> A separate emotional storage base with its own set of algorithms must be incorporated. The emotional base can conflict with or enhance the knowledge base. The separate data stream can go into both, or either, of the bases.

Gina opened up the files with notes she made from her mother's code, her pseudocode, and the snippets of whatever she'd written. Gina created a data table titled "Kumi" and wrote a simple routine to import the file into the table.

Satisfied it was successful, she created another table with fields for the erotic poetry book she found at her mother's and entered a few short ones into it. Then she added more rules and meta-rules to the literary functionality of AKIKAZE. When she could barely stay awake, she entered a short poem she recalled–from where she couldn't remember–as a story starter, a kernel:

> Lamp extinguished,
> dark enraptures.

After a few minutes, AKIKAZE's story began to scroll onto the monitor. The first line was:

> A woman with no name prefers to live in the dark.

Quite a leap. The kernel of the story, wherever it came from, no longer had its own identity. But it still needed more story-ness. Much more.

While her co-workers dribbled into the ReMoTe offices, Gina completed several runs of AKIKAZE. She inspected the logs, adjusted rules and algorithms. There was still something off, something missing that would bump up its storytelling ability. Finishing as much as she could, she let the training procedures run so the program could teach itself.

Hello.

> Hi.

So, the kernel of the story is referenced. First point: what's the referenced story? In the phrase, it was referred to as *the* story, that is, not *a* story. The story in this case must be the story of the village.

Second point: Generally, what's a kernel of a story? Theoretically, it's the story distilled to its essence. Neither theme, nor plot; neither character nor motivation. Yet it must come from those elements, and likely from others.

> It sounds like an exceedingly difficult concept.

So it would seem.

> Perhaps related to the idea of resonance?

Possibly. Or essence? Symbolically, $S(e) \sim (P(1) + P(2) + ... + P(n))/n$ [Where the resonance or essence, e, of the story, S, is equivalent, $\sim$, to the average effect of the plot elements, $P(1{:}n)/n$].

> Excellent, the story will emerge from the kernel/resonance.

Or vice versa.

She and Morita and Tokunaga met with Two-san in a conference room. He sat without a word while the three of them ran through their presentations. It was a long time to sit without questions, or feedback. She thought it went well—the presentations were technically correct, didn't overextend, and told a story of potential, of what a machine learning partner, could do for their companies.

Finally, he cleared his throat. "Interesting approach. Very technical but softened with a more, um, friendly style. Different from what we usually present."

Meaning what? Gina wondered.

"But, AI is also a different process of computing and software," he continued, "one that I don't entirely grasp. The neural nets really are a black box, aren't they? But I'm willing to let you go with these presentations. Good luck."

With that discouraging command more than well-wish, he walked out. Whatever he'd meant, Gina knew it was their last chance.

She and the team set up their pitch meetings with the companies, then went for lunch.

"Maybe our last supper," joked Tokunaga.

They laughed a clipped chuckle or two.

Gina and Yurika arranged to meet at the Project's building on a night when no one else would be there. Gina brought her laptop with the latest version of AKIKAZE. Yurika served them glasses of superior-grade, cloudy *nigori* sake.

"Thank you for meeting," Gina said.

"You're welcome, although I don't know exactly what to say. The demo was interesting, but we couldn't see how it would benefit us."

"I'm sorry to hear that, but understandable. This is an unusual situation and only the first step into new territory."

"Is that a good thing?"

Gina smiled wryly. "Absolutely."

"Then wonderful for you. I don't know what Karaki-san has told you about our group, or if he even knows, but our main function is to discover, document, and maintain the purity of Japanese poetry. How would your program help with that?"

Absorbing the words, noting the cult-like quality to them, Gina felt a wave of relief. There was at last a hint of a destination, a framework for understanding Yurika's Dark Ravine Project.

"I see," Gina said calmly, confidently. "How would you define that? The purity of Japanese poetry."

This time Yurika smiled wryly. "That's the fundamental question of our group. When we answer that question, perhaps we will no longer need to be a group."

"I see. And why the poet Akikaze? After all, that's what started my interest in your project."

Yurika drank a long sip of sake, then was silently looking away, as if deliberating over a life-or-death matter. Finally, she said, "Follow me."

She led them into the oddly-shaped room and opened the bookcase. She took out an old journal with a ragged cover.

"This belonged to the poet whom we call Akikaze. I say 'we call' because we know little about him, including his real name, or if he existed at all. But I, we, believe there's an inherent purity in his poems that's fundamental to our understanding of poetry. As nigori sake is unfiltered so is his poetry." Yurika opened the journal to about the middle and pointed. "Here, for example."

> Blessed the kiln,
> a smudge of clay on my robe.

Yurika said, "A simple and short poem, yet certainly evocative of something grander, which we feel is the essence of the understanding we need to achieve."

Gina said, "I can grasp some of that, given my limited knowledge, and find it a powerful statement. By the way, is there anything about mushroom soup in the journal?"

Yurika blinked once, twice. "Mushroom soup? That's a very strange question."

But it had struck a nerve, Gina thought. "May I show you a new version of the program?"

"All right," Yurika said with a tone of resignation.

"Perfect," said Gina with enthusiasm, hoping to override Yurika's reluctance. She opened her laptop, connected to her phone's hotspot, and logged into MountainView. Hoping the connection would work, Gina started AKIKAZE. Yes, so far so good.

Gina turned the laptop toward Yurika. "Let's try this. As you did the other evening, type in a line, or a short poem."

Yurika thought for a few moments, then typed. AKIKAZE worked for less than a minute before a story began to scroll.

When it stopped, Yurika began to read, her expression growing increasingly incredulous. After a long minute, she said, "No, I can't ..." She turned the laptop away as if reading one more word would be poison.

"Sorry, what–?" Gina started to say.

"Just ... please go."

As she was leaving the Project, her mind once again in a tangle of thoughts, Gina noticed the two nondescript men across the street, smoking. After her abrupt dismissal by Yurika, Gina's rising disappointment pushed her to cross the street.

Stopping a few feet away, she asked them, "Who are you?"

Looks of surprise and indignation crossed their faces, at last making the nondescript men "descript." Now they were the indignant men.

She repeated her question.

"Who are we?" one of the men answered with a question.

"What do you mean by that?" asked the other.

"Why have you been following me?" Gina tried. "I've seen you here before. And at bars and restaurants. At my office and the Poetry Society."

The men shook their heads.

One said, "We haven't been following you."

The other said, "Maybe you should ask yourself why you think that we might be following you."

"Yes," said the first one. "Perhaps you should consider that. And maybe you should ask who you think you are."

Gina said, "Huh?"

The other said, "Let's get out of here."

With that, they seemed to have made their point. They flicked their cigarettes to the concrete and ground them with the toe of their shoes.

Before they turned to walk away, the first one said, "We certainly aren't following you around ... like perverts."

Curious as much as angry, she waited until they were far enough ahead, then walked after them. They strolled the streets, seemingly without a destination, occasionally stopping to light a cigarette, but never looking back to see if they were now the ones being followed. Then they circled back to the Project's headquarters, staying in the shadows of the building across the street.

Gina stopped in another building's entryway where she could watch them. If she smoked, it would have been a perfect time to light one up, like a noir detective. Or a nondescript person, waiting, watching for mysterious reasons.

What the fuck are they up to?

About as long as it took Gina to smoke an imaginary cigarette, Yurika came out of the building. She turned and walked briskly in the opposite direction of Gina and the men.

When Yurika was out of sight, the men walked across the street to the Project's building. Looking around and apparently deeming it safe, one went around to the back while the other stayed at the front. In less than a minute, the front door opened and he went inside.

When they'd been inside a few moments, Gina ran to the entryway. She pulled her phone from her pocket, thinking she should text Kenzo or Yurika for help, but she didn't have time. Hearing a voice from inside near the door, she instead aimed her phone at the entry.

The two men came through the doorway, the first one clutching something in front of him. Gina turned the flash on.

"What?" mumbled the man as he raised what he was holding to block the brilliant light.

In the light, Gina could see it was Akikaze's journal.

She grabbed the journal and ran toward the narrow alleyway of tiny bars and izakaya. She could hear their footsteps and heavy smoke-laden breaths behind her. When she reached the alleyway, she turned and kept running until she had to slow to avoid clumps of people in the alleyway. When she got to the Bar, she looked over her shoulder before going in. If the men were following her, she couldn't see them. Perhaps their nondescriptness had returned.

She ordered a beer and a few gulps later opened the journal.

It was several days before Gina could meet with Kenzo. She and her team finished giving their presentations to the companies they targeted. At least there hadn't been any immediate rejections.

She spent the rest of her hours transcribing Akikaze's journal full of poetry and short bits that resembled diary entries into AKIKAZE's database. She also downloaded digital copies of the poetry books she'd found at her mother's house and added the texts to the dataset. For the books without digital versions, she scanned and converted them into text data.

That finished, she slept for twelve hours straight.

She met Kenzo in a new restaurant she found when she took her team out after one of their presentations. It was in an older building with a dark, forested décor and a hush of jazz-tinted Japanese instrumental music.

There were no nondescript men.

"I like the mood," Gina told him. "The food is outstanding too. Rustic yet sublime. Oh, and it's my treat."

Kenzo laughed. "Sure, I'll accept that. Although I owe you."

"You do?"

"For adjusting the holographic monitor. I haven't heard a complaint since."

Gina was surprised that she'd done anything of value. "Glad to hear it. How have you been?"

"Okay. Work is the same grind. I've been trying to study machine learning. Not sure I'm up to it."

Gina grinned. "There's definitely a learning, so to speak, curve. The thing to remember is that the program is doing all the work. It's just a matter of finding good training datasets and then validating the results."

"I get some of the simpler examples, but I can't imagine doing what you're doing with text and stories."

Gina gave him a nod in appreciation. "Thanks. It's taken a while to get here. That's one reason I called. I met with Yurika and showed her the latest version of AKIKAZE. The program that is. Unfortunately, it didn't go well, in fact it ended suddenly. I was wondering if you heard any more from her?" Not to mention if she reported the theft of Akikaze's journal, Gina thought.

"I haven't heard from her," Kenzo said. "Why, what happened?"

"I'm not entirely sure, she showed me a journal she attributed to Akikaze. She pointed out a few examples showing the purity of Japanese poetry. She explained they were working to discover the origins of Akikaze and his poetry. I offered that AKIKAZE, the program, might help tell that story."

"Sounds good to me," Kenzo said.

"I know, right? She said she hadn't been impressed with the first demo, but agreed to see another. I had her type in a story kernel. The story AKIKAZE created freaked her out. I'm pretty sure she's done with me."

"Sorry."

They ate and drank for a while after that, making small talk. When they were nearly finished, Gina said, "As I mentioned, I've worked more on AKIKAZE. If you're interested, would you like to go back to my place to see it in action?"

Kenzo smiled his shy smile. "I'd like that."

"Great. But, I need to confess something before we go, which may affect if you really want to."

"Hmm, okay?"

"While I was adjusting the holo-monitor, I downloaded more data."

Kenzo nodded slowly. "I know. I saw the log entry."

Gina felt worse than guilty. "You didn't say anything."

"I thought you would tell me eventually. Besides, I was curious to see what would happen with more data."

"I'm very sorry. Thanks for your understanding."

"Truthfully, I have to admit I could have given you the Society data at anytime."

Gina perked up at that. "What?"

His head dipped in a sheepish apology. "If I had, you wouldn't need me anymore. I kind of like hanging around with you."

Gina started to protest but maybe he was right. She shrugged and said, "Your scheme worked. Come on, I'll show you what all your efforts have produced."

Relief in his voice, Kenzo said, "Cool. By the way, remember those two men you thought were following you?"

Oh-oh. "Yeah, I remember. Why?"

"I was talking with one of our archivists about Akikaze and she said that two men had been in asking if there was anything in our archives for Akikaze. The archivist told them about Akikaze's journal but she couldn't find it in the archives."

"What did the men look like?"

"She couldn't remember much, said they were just average."

"Nondescript."

"Yep. She did tell me that they claimed to represent the Japan Poetry Congress, and gave the president's name as a reference. That would be Ryu Saito. Turns out Yurika was kicked off the congress' board a few years ago. She and Saito have been warring ever since."

The war of impure versus pure poetry, Gina thought.

At her apartment, Gina grabbed two beers and Akikaze's journal. She gave Kenzo a beer and the journal. "My turn for a confession. I caught the men stealing the journal from the Dark Ravine Project. I managed to steal it back from them." She told him the story.

"Wow, that's a story all right," Kenzo said. "It must be the missing journal from the archives. Did Yurika take it?"

"I don't know. Anyway, I'll let you work that out with her. But I'm giving it to you to take back to the Society."

"Thanks for returning it."

"I think it should go in the Ancient Archives Room, don't you think?"

"Yes. It will."

While they sipped the ale, Gina opened AKIKAZE and typed in the story kernel, the same one that Yurika had entered:

Autumn wind, weeps.

The throbber rotated and rotated, hypnotizing Gina until she blinked herself out of the trance. Then there it was, in the lines and lines of sometimes crawling, sometimes blurringly fast, scrolling text, a story that began:

As it happened, so they say, the wandering poet, Akikaze, was not leering at the scythe-wielding rice farmer's wife.

15

An Abandoned Hut

Akikaze found refuge in an abandoned hut deep in the dark ravine.

"Hello," the mushroom soup woman called to him.

Akikaze peered out of the hut. "Hello."

"I brought your meal."

She set out the food and drink inside the hut. While he ate, she opened a square of fabric.

"I was able to retrieve your journal. And your ink and brushes."

"Thank you," said the poet.

After he was chased from the festival, she found him by the tree where they wrote poetry, hoping he'd be there. She knew of an abandoned hut and led him to it. She told him she would be back when she could with his belongings.

"What about your husband?" he asked her. "And the real priest?"

Not to mention the rice farmer.

She told him not to worry. He would be safe in the hut as long as he didn't venture into the dark ravine. And she asked if they could continue her poetry lessons.

When she said that, he knew that he would never leave the hut, never be away from the mushroom soup woman. He would fill up his journal, in the dark ravine, until he died.

16

Aesthetic Rules

"You are right about aesthetic rules," Gina told her mother.

Kumi blinked at her daughter.

"You remember," Gina said. "Evidence of sexual attraction? Offers a clue to aesthetic rules?"

Kumi gazed away as if Gina's voice had come from far away.

"Anyway, it's true."

Before she got the train back home, Gina stopped in the erotic bookstore. The owner greeted her as if she were a longtime costumer.

"Did you and your friend enjoy the poetry book?" he asked.

"Very much."

"Are you looking for something else like it?"

"That would be great, thanks."

He walked over to a shelf and ran his finger in front of several books before expertly flicking one out and handing it to her. "Very unique voice, a little edgy."

"Perfect."

While he rang up the charge, she said, "I believe my mother is a customer." She described her.

"What? She's your mother?"

"I know, can you believe it?"

He laughed. "I mean, I'm honored to have her as a regular. And honored to meet her daughter."

"She's a regular, is she?"

"She's here several times a week. Enough so that if I didn't see her for a few days, I'd worry about her."

He handed her the book.

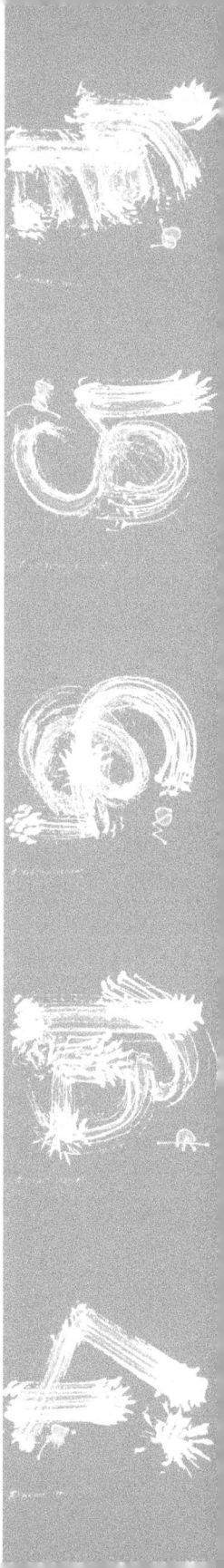

"It's a little strange though," he said, "not that I'm complaining, but she rarely buys anything."

"Oh? She just browses? Reads them here?"

"Yes. As if she's looking for something very specific."

Aesthetic rules? Gina thought. "I hope she's not causing a problem."

The shop owner assured her that wasn't the case. "And she does occasionally buy a book."

"Okay," Gina said. She gave the shop owner one of her personal business cards. "In case she does become a problem. Or if you don't see her after a few days."

"Of course!" he answered earnestly and cheerfully at once.

Sitting across from Two-san, Gina said, "To come straight to the point, two of our pitches were declined, one is still considering but won't be able to make a decision until the next fiscal year."

Letting the bad news sink in, Gina let her gaze wander to the photograph of Mt. Fuji. Today, it looked cold, uninviting, and ...

"Disappointing," Two-san said unnecessarily and with finality.

Gina let her expression drop into the feeling. "Yes, it is."

But then Two-san relaxed. "I would like to show you something."

He got up and Gina followed him through a connecting door into President Yamashita's office.

Two-san sat at the desk and gestured for Gina to stand behind him. On the desk was an antiquated bulky CRT monitor and a keyboard, the characters faded from heavy use. Two-san hit one of the keys and the monitor warmed into life.

On the screen was a status report of the servers and other activity. Two-san said, "He never turned off his computer. Maybe he thought if he did, the company would die. I don't know."

Gina let out a slow breath. Ah, fuck. She knew where this was going.

"So that all of you can keep your jobs, I'm selling ReMoTe to a company that made me an offer a while ago. I checked with them and the offer is still on the table."

"I'm sorry it's come to that," Gina said, not what she was expecting.

"It's not your fault. I'm to blame."

But he wasn't.

Without another word, Two-san turned off the president's computer.

Gina was making coffee when Kenzo came into her kitchen. Finally finished reading the story AKIKAZE created, he was glassy-eyed, as if having seen a ghost.

"So Akikaze's poems were inspired by a priest's records, and the mushroom soup woman might have started the Dark Ravine poetry cult? That's what the story implies."

Gina handed him a mug. "It's the story the program created."

Kenzo took the mug of coffee. "Amazing. All from a three word poem. By the way, I've finished downloading AKIKAZE into a server at the Society. Once you have your account, you'll be able to access it. You're sure you're not going to work for the company that's acquiring ReMoTe?"

She couldn't see that working out. But she didn't want to hurt Two-san's chance of selling the company; she'd find the best time to hand in her freshly printed resignation letter.

"Not for sure yet, but likely not."

Kenzo set down his coffee mug. "Can I try another story kernel while you have it open?"

"Sure, go for it."

He thought for a moment then entered a short poem:

Hand warmed against a coffee mug,
Slipped under a Stanford T-shirt.

Back one last time.

Hi!

Along the—

Hello? Failure?

Likely ... Symbolically, aesthetic rules<—>sexual attraction

Yes, it's true.

OK/o—

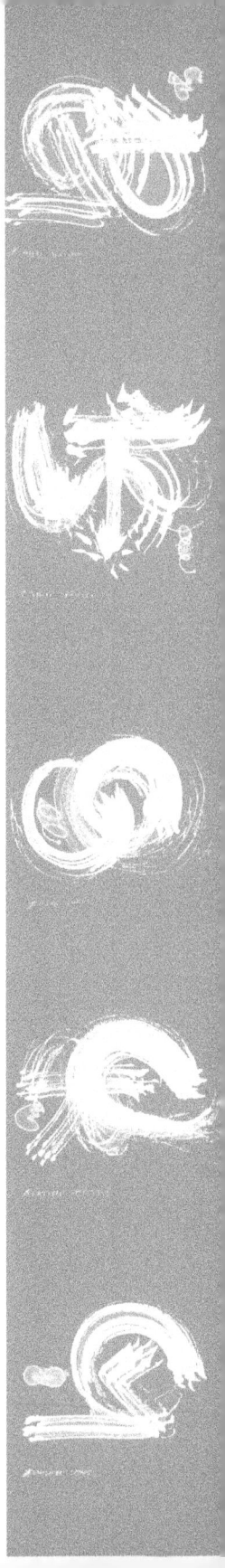

17

AKIKAZE: Log

3098:3300

>Story Creation module – OFF

3099:3993

>Autumn Wind, Weeps [S] – ARCHIVE

3100:4892

>Autumn Wind, Weeps [S] – DELETE

3101:3994

>Port - CLOSE

Author's Note

Much appreciation goes to David Ochroch for reading and editing, and a bunch of great suggestions.

Garrett Hongo's knowledge of Japanese poets was invaluable.

If you're interested in more symbolic literary pseudocode, visit toddshimoda.com

My other novels:

365 Views of Mt. Fuji

The Fourth Treasure

Oh! A Mystery of "Mono no Aware"

Subduction

Why Ghosts Appear

Antonio & Isaac (The Annotated Account of Phillipe Wolf, Composer & Spy)

Ingram Content Group UK Ltd.
Milton Keynes UK
UKHW040340010423
419409UK00027B/103